PENGUIN METRO BOOK

VISHWAMITRA

Dr Vineet Aggarwal is a doctor by qualification, manager by profession and artist by temperament. Born in a family of doctors, he successfully completed an initial stint with the family occupation before deciding to venture into pharmaceutical management. He pursues writing as a passion and is an avid travel photographer as well.

His literary repertoire extends from politics to poetry and travel to terrorism but his favourite genre remains the amalgamation of science and mythology. He is the author of the popular online blogs Decode Hindu Mythology and Fraternity Against Terrorism and Extremism. This is his first book.

VISHWAMITRA

DR VINEET AGGARWAL

Penguin
metro reads

An imprint of Penguin Random House

PENGUIN METRO READS

USA | Canada | UK | Ireland | Australia
New Zealand | India | South Africa | China | Singapore

Penguin Metro Reads is part of the Penguin Random House group of companies
whose addresses can be found at global.penguinrandomhouse.com

Published by Penguin Random House India Pvt. Ltd
4th Floor, Capital Tower 1, MG Road,
Gurugram 122 002, Haryana, India

Penguin
Random House
India

First published in Penguin Metro Reads by Penguin Books India 2014

Copyright © Dr Vineet Aggarwal 2014

All rights reserved

10 9 8 7 6 5 4 3 2

ISBN 9780143423447

Typeset in Minion Pro by Eleven Arts, New Delhi

Printed at Repro India Limited

www.penguin.co.in

To
My grandparents, who introduced me to the world of mythology,
My father, the epitome of truth and kindness,
My mother, the ray of light in my life,
and
My sister, who taught me the power of a pen

Contents

Author's Note
The Friend of the World

For any writer, his first book holds special value since it is as much a labour of love and sweat as an exercise in discovering one's own latent potential and this book is my labour of love and sweat in more ways than one.

Vishwamitra isn't a religious book, nor a book on spirituality. It's neither completely fiction nor entirely based on reality. Yet, it holds an important message, for it is the life story of an ordinary human who rose above the confines of his physical and mental boundaries to fight fate and take charge of his own destiny.

Unlike the Devas, Gandharvas, Vidyadhars, Siddhas, Arihants, Bodhisattvas and other assorted divine beings from our scriptures, we, the ordinary Manavs (the Sanskrit term for Man) are considered to have limited capabilities. Yet, we see people in a variety of disciplines seeking to breach that barrier every day. These are the people who challenge the norms set by the society and set new milestones for the rest of mankind. This story is an ode to one such man.

Vishwamitra's life is the perfect example of how far a man can go in order to obtain what he truly desires. Many may know of him as one of the greatest rishis of Vedic times and some may even remember the role he plays in the Ramayana. But even those who are familiar with his name may not know that Vishwamitra was born a prince and became a Brahmarishi purely by virtue of his own efforts. You may be further surprised to know that he is also the discoverer of the Gayatri Mantra, the most popular hymn chanted by millions of Hindus all over the globe every day.

The characters of this book may remind you of people from our own lives since human emotions haven't changed since the time the first of mankind walked out of Africa. Yet, the views expressed by the central character may seem untraditional and even heretical at times, for he does not see the world through the prism of established religious doctrines.

Born into a Kshatriya family, divine providence blessed him with a potent spiritual streak that fuelled his quest to become the highest of the high priests of ancient India. History identifies him as the only Kshatriya king to have achieved the impossible task of becoming a Brahmarishi and recognizes him as the human architect of no less than a star system!

His story isn't confined to a study of human psychology or mythology but rather takes on the mantle of science fiction more than once, bringing to the fore universal traits that can be found in any intelligent species in the universe. You may believe everything, or take it with a pinch of salt, but either way, you would find it hard not to be impressed with the man's steadfast dedication to his goal and the absolute brilliance of his methodology.

This book is a chronicle of the trials and tribulations faced by a man torn between duty and desire, and the vicissitudes and failings of human condition. Yet, at its heart, it is a story of hope—hope that makes a human being challenge his destiny with random acts of free will; hope that makes a king leave all his possessions and turn into a hermit; hope that fuels the desire for being remembered in spirit, even after the body has perished in dust.

This, thus, is the narrative of a brave king of Aryavarta, who not only attained fame through his military conquests but, through his intense spiritual quest, also became one of the most well-known sages of all time.

It is the story of a man who dared to challenge the gods.

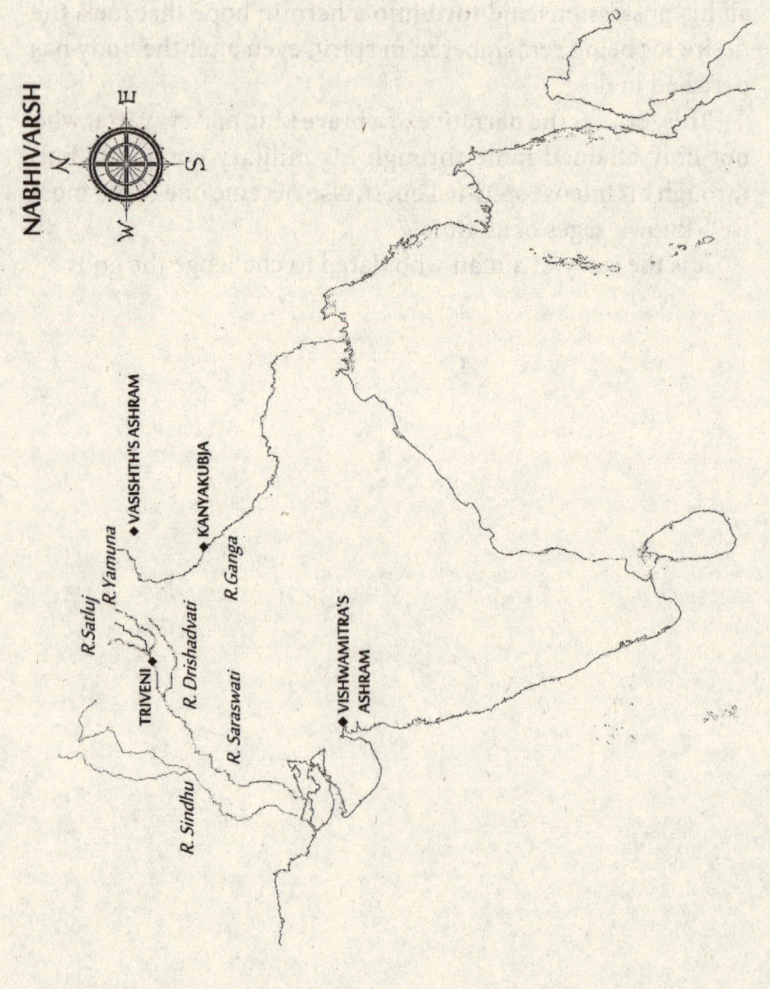

Prologue: Before the Beginning

He woke up as if from a deep slumber, his eyes adjusting to the darkness as he tried to make sense of what was around him.

He seemed to be sitting on a giant flower whose name he did not know.

Lotus . . . it was as if someone had whispered the name in his ear.

What colour was it that appealed so much to his senses?

Golden . . . the voice said.

So he was sitting on a gold-coloured lotus, he surmised.

But then his bewilderment grew as he realized that even though he now knew where he was sitting, he still did not know his own name.

Brahma . . . the voice whispered this time.

It told him he was the First Mortal Being in this new world and the Creator of all other creatures that would follow. Incredible! That sounded like a massive task considering that until a moment ago, he had not even known who he was. He started to scratch his head and ran into an unexpected obstruction. There seemed to be four of them!

Lowering his eight eyes, he examined himself critically. His body had six long appendages—four on the upper half and two

1

below his waist. He realized he could stand on the lower two and use the upper four to balance himself. He used two of them to feel his face and get an idea of how he looked.

There seemed to be four weirdly shaped protuberances on top of his torso, each looking in different directions through two apertures. He closed all but two of them and realized that when he did that, his vision was limited to one direction. As he opened all the apertures on his four faces, he got a 360 degree view all around him though he could only see darkness as far as his vision permitted.

A million questions bubbled in his mind. What did Brahma mean? Why was he all alone? Whose was this voice giving him directions? What did he want him to create? Should he even do what the voice said?

A deep rumble began to fill the darkness and he heard a monosyllabic sound: *OM*.

OM?

What did that mean? What sort of a word was that?

OMMMM . . . the voice said again and he felt his questions dissolving in its unfathomable depth. He sat down on the huge petals of the golden lotus. The incantation continued and he felt himself compelled to say it himself.

'Ommmm . . . ' he uttered, hearing his own voice for the first time.

It sounded pleasing, almost like a fleeting reflection of the voice that had told him his name and purpose. He kept repeating the word and it seemed more comprehensible with each repetition.

It was the sound of creation manifesting by the will of God.

It started with an A, the first sound to come out of a mouth struggling to form words; bent itself around a lingering U, stretching on itself, reflecting the space–time continuum; and ended with an M, the sound created by a closing mouth thereby encompassing all possible words that could be formed by opening and closing his mouth.

He felt a deep calm engulf his being and realized this primeval syllable had emanated from none other than the mind of Narayan, the One who lay in water, at the bottom of this egg-shaped universe. It was He who had informed him about being the first mortal being in this universe. His sharp mind understood the unsaid implication—that Narayan was the Immortal One and existed before him and would do so even after he ceased to exist.

He saw a vision of Narayan, lying on a huge coiled being at the bottom of the universe. His blue body glowed with a radiance so brilliant that Brahma had to shield his eyes with trembling hands. The Lord had four upper appendages and two lower ones as well. That gave him comfort, since he was obviously made in the reflection of the Maker.

The long coiled being on which the Lord lay had a thousand bobbing heads with beaded eyes that glared at Brahma impassively. They put the fear of Death in his mind and he gulped nervously. The serpent was Time, the end of all worlds, but Brahma had no cause to worry for he was just beginning his journey, the last step towards salvation.

As he understood this Eternal Truth, Brahma felt all his anxiety disappear. The purpose of creation was revealed to him. He would create immovable and movable objects to sustain the millions of souls who had lost direction and were looking for a way to reach home.

Home . . . the abode of Narayan.

That was where he belonged. That was where everyone belonged. And he had been chosen for this specific task from amongst the teeming millions based on his previous life's Karma.

Karma . . . It was what it all boiled down to.

One's actions and their consequences formed an intricate web that bound every living soul in this world to every other living being. And they would keep taking birth again and again to balance out these transactions till they were free of the debt they owed each other.

Samsar . . . That was what this unending circle of life and death was called.

He had managed to free himself from this cycle to almost the highest limit a living being could and had been chosen for the role of Brahma. He realized with a twinge of guilt that he could have completely bypassed this birth had he put in a little more effort to be free.

Be that as it may, he needed to focus on the task at hand and fulfil it to the best of his abilities so that he could get rid of this material body in this birth itself. He had a hundred years to live, each year filled with 360 days and the same number of nights.

His excitement grew as he realized what lay ahead of him. His mind was already bursting with ideas that seemed too fancy. He imagined building light points in the darkness and calling them stars. There would be clusters of these stars in various formations and together they would fill this universe with a warm glow.

Each star would have smaller globes circling it on which different souls would find a place to reside and fulfil their Karma. The panch mahabhoot would be his building blocks and he was free to try various permutations and combinations and create beings that dwelt in water, air, fire or anyplace at all, as per his desire.

Names started popping into his head as he thought of what all he would create—small unicellular beings that would clump and divide resulting in various other, higher life forms that could breathe, work, sleep, eat, reproduce and strive for salvation just like him. Plants and animals, humans and nymphs, dinosaurs and dragons, demons and demigods . . . The possibilities were endless and he rubbed his hands in glee.

There would be families, dynasties and kingdoms; civilizations, empires and interstellar alliances; avarice, altruism and ambition; monsters, mysticism and machines; politics, propriety and philosophy; and of course lust, love and wars.

Brahma, the First Mortal Being of the Universe, was ready.

It was time to begin the beginning.

Satyavati

Adhyaye 1

Sunlight streamed through the latticework, creating patterns on the thick rug below his feet. Sparrows chirped on the windowsill and the fragrance of lotus blooms suffused the air. Kadhi, the king of Mahodayapur, anxiously paced outside his wife's bedchamber.

As he came to a halt at the window, the soft northern wind blew his curly hair away from his high forehead, revealing an angular yet handsome face with deep-set hazel eyes, an aquiline nose and a strong, determined jawline. A scar cut across his left cheek and ended just below the earlobe—remnant of the victory he had obtained against the barbaric hordes of the west.

He wondered why, despite all his royal accomplishments, the personal lives of his family had not been that great. For reasons best known to the gods, they had not been very lucky in terms of an heir. Ghritachi was an Apsara who had fallen in love with a mortal, his father, Prince Kushanabh. Though the king and queen had given their blessings to the young couple, destiny, as was generally observed, had its own plans.

The human–nymph pairing could only produce daughters, since Apsaras could only give birth to Apsaras. While the daughters were beautiful, blessed with their mother's looks, they were also a proud lot, perhaps for the very same reason.

When approached by Vayu, the lord of air, with a marriage proposal, they refused as they believed they deserved someone even better. Enraged, the fierce Vayu decided to teach them some humility and cursed them to lose their looks and become hunchbacks. The royal family drowned in sorrow and the capital city came to be known as Kanyakubja, the city of hunchbacked maidens.

Kushanabh was devastated but decided to seek divine intervention. He consulted the high priests and convinced them to organize a Putra-kaam-eshti Yagnya to propitiate the gods and bless him with an heir.

Thus was born Kadhi, a bouncy baby boy blessed by no less than Indra himself.

And now that his wife was expecting, he just wanted a healthy child and did not care whether it was a boy or a girl. He did not have to wait long. Soon the cries of the newborn filled the palace and turned the anxious environment cheerful in an instant.

Almost immediately, the intricately carved teak doors of the bedchamber opened and two maids came running towards him with the good news. His queen had given birth to a beautiful and healthy baby, fair like the jasmine flowers blooming in his garden.

Kadhi was beside himself with joy and rewarded the maids with two of his most cherished rings. Having been dealt a cruel blow by the gods of fate before, his adoptive parents had worried if he would ever be blessed with a child himself. Nothing would give them more pleasure than the news that his wife and newborn child were healthy and the lineage of his adoptive forefathers would go on.

He entered the queen's chamber, instructing the maids to share the good news with his parents and the rest of the royal family. As he ran to his wife's bedside, the other maids took a step back and melted into the shadows to give the royal family a moment of privacy.

Kadhi hugged his wife, setting eyes on his daughter for the first time.

The infant lay next to her mother, wrapped in soft muslin. Her rosy cheeks were stained with tears and the toothless mouth was still complaining to the skies.

He picked her up gingerly and looked into her deep-brown eyes. Tears of joy fell from his eyes and he quietly made a resolve to himself. He would groom his daughter as the heir to his kingdom, regardless of her gender.

He would break the curse on his family and turn their luck around.

Adhyaye 2

'Satyavati!'

Kadhi called out as he entered Rani Mahal, the palace of queens.

Any of the hundred palace maids could have summoned the princess but he waved them away. Though a stickler for protocol in the Raj Bhavan, when at home he liked to have a semblance of a normal family life and spend time with his wife and daughter.

Sometimes he felt he had not devoted enough time to Satyavati, for it seemed like just yesterday that the little bundle of joy had so vociferously announced her arrival in their palace.

What had followed was a festival the likes of which had not been seen in Mahodayapur before. The royal family had been relieved that no genetic defects were found in the baby and called for a celebration inviting the neighbouring kings to the gala.

Kulguru Dhanu had named her Satyavati, the one who imbibes truth, and as she grew up Kadhi made sure she received the education and military training a male heir would have. Lately, he had started getting the feeling that the time to crown her was not far and, before that happened, he wanted to spend as much time with her as his duties to the kingdom would allow.

As he turned a corner, he saw her walking towards him gracefully.

He found a reflection of his wife's beauty in his daughter's face. Thick lashes gave definition to deep-brown doe eyes and her bronze skin and high cheekbones painted a pretty picture. An emerald-green angavastra was draped around her athletic body in a manner that would allow easy movement, unlike the garments worn by the other princesses in the palace. Her hand rested on the hilt of the dagger tied to her waist.

Queen Ratna accompanied her. She was dressed in regal finery that would make the Apsaras in Indra's court envious and looked like a slightly older version of Satyavati. King Kadhi loved the two ladies in his life and was thankful to God that they both loved him back with equal devotion.

As Satyavati came running into his arms he felt pride in having been blessed with such an obedient and loving child. Kadhi gestured to the guards and maids to leave them alone and the trio walked leisurely towards the small lake full of lavender water lilies and snow-white swans.

Every evening, the small family spent time by the water, talking about things that could enhance Satyavati's education, yet would not seem too boring. In the afternoon, she would hear stories about their glorious Chandravanshi ancestors from her grandfather and in the evening would ask her father to fill in the details that may have been missed.

Today, she wanted to know more about Jahnu, a much-talked-about ancestor, who had conducted the Sarva-medham Yagnya for the benefit of mankind. Legend had it that Goddess Ganga had desired him as a husband but was refused by the ascetic king. Grandfather Kushanabh had ended the story at that point but Satyavati knew there was more to it.

She coaxed her father to continue and the king was more than happy to oblige. He thought for a few moments about how to present the story to his young, impressionable daughter and then began, 'All right, so Jahnu refused Ganga's wedding proposal on the grounds that he had become an ascetic but Ganga was tumultuous and wont to have her own way. When her mighty waters could break boulders into gravel what was the will of a mere human!

'While the great yagnya was being performed, Ganga altered her normal course and rushed towards the yagnyasthala, the ritual site, in order to flood the area and disrupt his sacrifice.'

Satyavati was surprised; she had always thought of the river as a mother who rid the world of its sins but then, she acknowledged, there could have been a bit of rebellion in the goddess when she was younger.

Meanwhile Kadhi continued animatedly, 'When Jahnu saw the entire yagnyasthala being flooded on purpose, he lost his cool. Highly offended at this intrusion, he summoned the mystical powers of his tapasya and drank the entire river.'

Both Ratna and Satyavati gave a start. An entire river swallowed by a human with mystical powers? Who would have thought!

Kadhi looked at their expressions and chuckled softly. 'Don't take the story too literally, my dears. I am sure the rishi must have used his siddhis to delude the goddess into believing what he wanted her to, in order to teach her a lesson. After all, there is a limit to one's physical capacity but none to the powers of the mind.'

Satyavati nodded softly. Yes, that sounded more plausible but then you never knew with these rishis! They had such mastery over their physical environment that they could easily perform the feats impossible for ordinary mortals.

'When the river goddess pleaded for mercy, Jahnu released her conditionally, admonishing her not to force her will on anyone again. He told her she was destined to obtain a great king as a husband and blessed her, saying that she would give birth to a son who would change Aryavarta forever. That prophesy is yet to be fulfilled and perhaps we may be witness to it in our lifetimes,' Kadhi declared with a dreamy look.

Sighing, he continued, 'Whatever the future holds, let us finish the stories of the past for now. Since Jahnu had given a sort of rebirth to the river, she was thenceforth referred to as Jahnavi. The great yagnya was completed and Jahnu returned to his kingdom. His subjects requested him for an heir and, to fulfil his duty to his people, Jahnu married Kaveri, another river goddess.'

At this point the queen added, 'Some say it was Ganga herself who took the form of Kaveri since she was still infatuated with the ascetic who had broken her pride. Whatever the truth, Kaveri is still known as Dakshin Ganga and the story of Ganga and Jahnu is famous amongst my people living along its banks.'

Kadhi rubbished it as a fairy tale but Satyavati was lost in deep thought.

How potent could a woman's determination be in changing the course of history! Had Ganga not flooded the yagnyasthala, Jahnu would not have blessed her with the promise that the future held. Who knew what that future would be? Suddenly she got goosebumps from the excitement coursing through her veins.

'Father,' she said timidly, 'Grandfather has told me the story of our forefathers, the great kings Ikshvaku, Nabhag, Jahnu and Pururavas. Each of them has stories that inspire one to achieve something stupendous in life. My training is proceeding well and however boring they may be, I am learning the scriptures diligently. But when will the time come for me to actually put all of this to use?'

Kadhi and Ratna smiled at this expression of impatience.

The king put his hand on Satyavati's head and said, 'My dear child, I know you are a master of horse riding but you need to hold your horses for now!'

He ruffled her hair and said lovingly, 'Most fathers think only of finding suitable grooms for their lovely daughters but your mother and I have never worried about that aspect. We have only dreamt of grooming you into a person perfectly capable of taking her own decisions as and when she feels right.'

Satyavati looked at his face intently and tried to read the emotions coursing through his mind. Kadhi said, 'Truth be told, I have been thinking on these lines for a while now and I only await the kulguru's return from Kashi to discuss with him the propitious time for conducting a ceremony to this effect.'

Satyavati's big brown eyes shone with happiness though her words were more measured 'Father, I am humbled that you think so highly of my capabilities. Your words have given me great encouragement and I promise to fulfil all expectations you and mother have of me!'

She bowed down to touch the feet of her parents and Queen Ratna hugged her tightly with tears of joy in her eyes.

'How fast you have grown, my child!' the queen said. 'I am proud of all the effort you have put into becoming the brave, strong and independent young woman that you are and I am sure you will achieve great milestones in your life ahead.

'While other princesses have wasted their time flirting with the royal princes of our nation and beyond, you have single-mindedly focused on achieving your goal. I daresay this trait comes from my side of the family!' she ended with a wink.

Kadhi smiled and declared, 'I agree with my dear queen in that respect. The time is not far when you will hold the reigns of this kingdom in your hands and I will sit by your side, watching you make wise decisions and fight wars. Together, we shall increase the glory of our kingdom and make our citizens the most prosperous in all of Nabhivarsh.'

The sun was setting by the time they started walking back and the trio felt deeply content.

It was rare for all members of a family, especially a royal one, to have the same goal in life and it was fortuitous that their desires intertwined. They would be lucky if they could bring their collective dream to fruition.

Adhyaye 3

The royal court of Kanyakubja was in session.

Supported by massive pillars of green marble, the circular hall spread in a wide arc and resembled an amphitheatre more than a private assembly. All were allowed admission, since the kingdom trusted its citizens and the need to provide security from the populace was never even considered.

The hall had a dome-shaped high roof which protected the occupants from the elements. It was painted midnight blue and decorated with the progressive phases of the moon, waxing and waning in endless succession.

Kadhi belonged to the Chandravansh, the lunar dynasty, hence the moon motif was abundant in all royal buildings. The hall was Vastu compliant; on the south-western end was a raised pedestal for the royal throne—a huge kneeling elephant carved out of black onyx, its trunk raised in salutation to the gods, bearing a towering howdah made of white marble and encrusted with blue emeralds on its back. On this unique throne, wearing a tall silver crown and peacock-blue royal garments, sat Kadhi. He had come to the court in great spirits but was in a sour mood now.

He had wanted to initiate the shift of power to his daughter after talking to the kulguru but the discussion had put a damper on his ambitions. The royal priest had suggested he wait for some time before announcing the coronation but had refused to explain why.

To spoil his mood further, he had just had to declare harsh punishment for a man who had robbed a friend of his life's savings. The court was applauding his decision for there was no place in a Chandravanshi kingdom for crime of any nature but Kadhi himself was disturbed.

What had he not provided to his subjects that they resorted to such actions? Mahodayapur was perhaps one of the most prosperous kingdoms in Nabhivarsh, or Aryavarta as they called it colloquially.

Kanyakubja was wealthy and its citizens prosperous. Temples, palaces, community halls, public baths, granaries, amphitheatres and fragrant gardens graced various parts of the city. He had built wide roads and avenues in all quarters of the kingdom and had had wells dug up and trees planted all along the highways. Taxes were fair, with every earning citizen paying ten per cent of their income in cash or kind to the royal treasury. The soil was fertile—a result of Mother Ganga's blessings—and Lord Indra had been especially merciful with the rains for almost a decade now.

Gurukuls existed in all four corners of the kingdom and children of all castes attended the ones falling in their quadrant. Since his mother was an Apsara, Kadhi had also encouraged scholarships towards the development of the arts. Musicians, dancers, sculptors, scribes and other artists were provided financial assistance and training to pursue their dreams so that people could enjoy their work and not just do it for the sake of earning money.

He wondered how, even with all this positive energy in his kingdom, crime could still exist. Civilization could only thrive if people rose above their individual greed and thought about society as a whole. Yet, it was so easy for mankind to return to its barbaric roots and destroy in a day what was built over decades.

His brooding was disturbed by an announcement. A rishi of impressive personality and indeterminate age was advancing towards the royal hall.

Sages were greatly venerated in Aryavarta and the page boys had hurriedly conveyed the news of his arrival the moment he had crossed the palace threshold. By the time the rishi entered the hall, Kadhi was at the entrance waiting for him with folded hands.

Rishi Ruchik was the son of the legendary Rishi Chyavan, who had distilled the essence of staying youthful and created a potion to that effect—the Chyavanprash. Rumour had it that the son was as talented as the father and would certainly perform great deeds in the future.

Kadhi led the rishi to a seat beside the throne reserved for visiting dignitaries and washed his feet, calling for refreshments. Only after the sage had been properly attended to did he ask the purpose of his visit.

Ruchik seemed embarrassed by all the attention and said, 'Rajan, I am pleased with the courtesy you have shown even though we have not personally met before. All the good things I have heard about you and your glorious ancestors today stand proven true. I bless you and your family with eternal happiness.'

Kadhi beamed with pleasure and bowed his head. 'My lord, it is the duty of a king to protect and serve sages and ascetics, for how else can his kingdom progress materially and spiritually? By the blessings of rishis like you, my kingdom is prosperous and happy. How can I not regard you with devotion?'

Ruchik nodded and smiled. 'It is this magnanimity that I had heard about that has brought me here today. I wish to ask of the king a gift so precious that a lesser man would refuse it outright.'

Kadhi was surprised. 'My lord, what is so precious that a king would not honour the request of a sage as venerated as yourself? I would gift you my entire kingdom if you so desired.'

The rishi shook his head. 'No, my king, I do not wish to deprive the kingdom of your astute leadership. You have continued the good work of your ancestors and the citizens are happier than they have ever been before.

'What I wish for requires a sacrifice that is more personal in nature and I would not have demanded it had my father not urged me to perform this task.'

For the first time a creeping suspicion began to take shape in Kadhi's mind. Ruchik noticed the furrowed brow and addressed Kadhi in a softer tone, 'My king, I am not here to make you uncomfortable but to request a favour that can only benefit you and your family in the long run. Fate had ordained that I come here and put before you the proposal that will change the future of your clan forever.'

Kadhi spoke cautiously, 'My father has taught me never to fight the flow of fate. Whatever you desire, O learned sage, I shall be glad to provide, irrespective of the personal cost involved.'

The rishi nodded in approval and said, 'Hear me then, Rajan. I, Ruchik, the son of Maharishi Chyavan and the grandson of Brahma's son Bhrigu, ask for the hand of your daughter, Satyavati, in marriage.'

The entire assembly was stunned into silence with this declaration for it was no secret that Princess Satyavati was to be crowned the king-in-waiting in a matter of days.

Kadhi was shocked and didn't know how to respond. Rishi Ruchik had been gentle in asking for the hand of his beloved daughter but had also conveyed his superior position by linking himself to the Creator. If he dared refuse him, Ruchik could very well reduce him to ashes right there or, worse still, put a curse on his daughter just like Vayu had put on his elder sisters!

He couldn't believe the sudden turn of events. Just a few moments ago he had been planning to retire and make his worthy daughter the sovereign of the kingdom and now all his dreams—rather, all their dreams—seemed to be crashing. How could he let his young and beautiful daughter marry this rishi and then send her off to the jungle?

Trying to think of a way to get out of the current predicament, he hit upon an idea.

Aloud he said, 'I would be happy to oblige you, Rishivar, but your request has put me in a deep dilemma.'

He sighed heavily before uttering the next words since they went against his deepest instincts.

'Chandravanshis have an ancient custom that only a man who can provide a thousand horses as white as the moon, each with one black ear, can marry the eldest princess of the household. I cannot ask this of a sage like you, nor can I refuse you my daughter. Hence, my mind is in turmoil.'

Ruchik's brow creased in thought but he replied in a non-committal tone, 'My king, when the Ashwini Kumars blessed my father with eternal youth, he had to conduct a yagnya to help them obtain Som Ras against the wishes of Indra. I understand this is the way of the material world; if one wants to obtain something he has to pay a price. Rest assured, I shall find a way to circumvent this condition without causing you any more anguish.'

Saying so, Ruchik got up from his seat and, with a curt nod to the king and the kulguru, marched out of the hall.

Kadhi did not bother to go back to the throne; he slowly sat down on the steps with his head in his hands.

Kulguru Dhanu walked closer to him and patted his shoulder. 'Rajan, I understand the situation you have been put in is not an easy one but it is the duty of a king to look after the well-being of his subjects more than his own family. If you anger Ruchik now, not only you and your family but the entire kingdom may be subject to his wrath.'

Kadhi bowed his head in submission. 'I understand the gravity of the situation, Gurudev, so I did not refuse the rishi outright. But how can I give the hand of my only child to a man who stays in the jungle like a nomad! From her birth Satyavati has been groomed into becoming the leader of her people and now this ascetic wants to take her away and subject her to a life of ignominy, discomfort and pain!

'I presented the only solution that came to my mind, an impossible condition, hoping that it would safeguard the future of not only my daughter but also of my subjects. Perhaps the love of one's own family and people is motive enough for one to commit a crime, however petty it may seem to some. I resorted to a lie, committed a sin and still may not have achieved anything!' he lamented.

Acharya Dhanu held the king by his shoulders and pulled him to his feet. 'Stand up, my king, and confront the challenge that stares you in the face. Do not lose hope for even though we humans do not have control over our destiny, the gods are merciful; surely, they have a plan for Satyavati and your kingdom.'

Kadhi looked at the Acharya who, for some mysterious reason, had a smile on his face.

'Let me assure you, Rajan, that the events that unfolded in the Raj Sabha today shall change the destiny of your kingdom for all time to come. Rishi Ruchik was sent here by his father and I suggest you consult your own father before taking any further action,' he ended cryptically.

Adhyaye 4

Satyavati heard the news of what had transpired in the Raj Sabha as she came out of her morning martial practice.

Her high cheekbones had a: touch of pink: more pronounced from her recent exertion but her ordinarily clear brow was furrowed because of what she had heard. She knew her father must be as devastated as she was with the demand of the rishi, however venerable he was.

She immediately ran to her grandfather's chambers where her father had been seen heading earlier. Her mind in turmoil, she burst into the large airy room where her grandparents lived, waving the guards aside and surprising the three elders gathered there.

Grandfather Kushanabh was well advanced in age but retained a handsome visage. His upright body bore signs of the numerous wars he had waged to establish the kingdom of Mahodayapur after his father, the great king Kush, had urged his four sons to carve out their own territories to rule rather than break the kingdom into four.

Grandmother Ghritachi, on the other hand, was an Apsara and so was unaffected by the mortal afflictions that bothered ordinary human beings. Her skin still radiated the beauty of a young woman and, looking at her, Satyavati often wondered how well she herself would age. In spite of their external differences, her grandparents were inseparable and everyone around had learnt to accept the incongruity in their appearance as a matter of fact.

Her father had been in deep conversation with them and she requested their permission to join the discussion. He seemed to have regained some of his composure and Satyavati knew whatever advice he gave would be in the best interests of Mahodayapur. To her astonishment though, her grandparents seemed delighted with the way things had turned out!

Kushanabh explained with a smile, 'My dear, you are surprised because you do not know the events that occurred before the gods bestowed your father upon us. What transpired in court today is simply a culmination of the events that took place after your aunts were cursed to become hunchbacks and our city drowned in sorrow.'

Now this sounded exciting, Satyavati thought.

Kadhi looked perplexed but Ghritachi came to his rescue, 'Dear boy, don't get caught up in your father's dramatics. Let me explain to you what had happened in the days that were like hell for our entire family.'

She paused to collect her thoughts before she spoke. 'As you both can imagine, Kushanabh and I were deeply troubled after Vayu dev cursed our daughters. Our once beautiful girls were disfigured and no one wanted to marry them any more. They were physically limited by their deformity and could not even help your father in the running of the kingdom.

'In those gloomy days, we were visited by Rishi Chyavan.'

Kadhi listened to the story in rapt attention, like a schoolboy. He had thought he knew everything worth knowing about his ancestors but turned out he didn't know enough about his own adoptive parents!

Ghritachi continued, 'Maharishi told your father that he had taken up a special vow for the welfare of the world and had come for help. Both of us were happy to serve such a revered personality and we thought perhaps his blessings would help us tide over the difficult time.

'The first night itself, he lay down in our bed, asking us to press his feet while he fell asleep. While this in itself is not an unreasonable demand, what became preposterous was that the rishi did not wake up for twenty-one consecutive days and neither of us dared get up for fear of waking him!'

Now *that* was something, Kadhi thought; the sage was surely testing his parents' patience.

Kushanabh took up the story, 'While your mother managed to do it since she has superhuman tolerance, I needed to take a break and also look after my kingdom's affairs! Yet, we both persevered since we had promised to help the Maharishi fulfil his vows.

'At the end of twenty-one days, Rishi Chyavan abruptly woke up and started walking briskly out of the palace. We tried to keep pace with him but were in bad shape because of lack of food and sleep. When we managed to catch up to him, he turned around and said, "O king, get your chariot ready, I want to see the city. And I want you and your wife to take the position of the horses and take me around,"' Kushanabh ended emotionally.

Satyavati realized the pain of those days still tormented her grandfather. Ghritachi patted his back and continued the tale. 'The royal council and of course both of us were stunned by this demand. But we had made a promise and were bound to fulfil the sage's every wish. Your father made all the arrangements and we both took position at the head of the chariot while Rishi Chyavan became the charioteer.'

She paused for a bit remembering the experience. 'While we were pulling the chariot, he used a thorny whip to prod us but we did not protest and continued to the best of our abilities. The onlookers were shocked and rushed forward to help us but the rishi waved them all away. This was a task that only we were supposed to do.'

Kadhi was shocked upon hearing of such mistreatment and his blood boiled with anger. Satyavati held her grandmother's hand and comforted her, trying to imagine the tribulations she must have gone through. For her, bearing all these misfortunes must have been more difficult for she had lived a long life of luxury in Indra's court before deciding to marry a human!

It was a tribute to the greatness of their love that they had never let their family even glimpse the burden on their own souls.

Kushanabh noticed their reactions and said, 'Let bygones be bygones, my children. Do not be affected by the events of the past for each of them has left us more equipped to deal with the future. Don't forget, it was only through these efforts that we could finally please the sage and he showed us the way to obtain an heir!'

Ghritachi resumed the story. 'The dreary part is over so cheer up, darlings,' she said, smiling. 'When we finally managed to drag the rishi back into the palace, he unyoked us from the chariot and both of us collapsed on the ground. He asked us to close our eyes and knelt beside us, placing a hand each on our heads.'

Her voice was now full of enthusiasm. 'You remember, my liege, the relief that coursed through our bodies? In an instant, both of us felt rejuvenated!'

Kushanabh nodded with a faint smile. 'A feeling of absolute bliss it was. It felt as if all my fatigue and shame were gone in an instant, replaced by a peace I had never felt before. He left us then and asked us to meet him the next day at dawn at the riverbank.'

For the first time during the conversation, Kadhi mustered control over his emotions and asked, 'But, father, why did the rishi put you through such an ordeal? What was the purpose of making a king and queen stoop to the level of beasts of burden? More importantly, why did you not protest?'

Kushanabh turned sombre and explained to his son, 'Kadhi, my boy, rishis are spiritually advanced beings who have reached that stage through a lifetime of perseverance. When they decide to bless someone they first make sure that the potential candidate is worthy of their benediction. Your mother and I knew that Rishi Chyavan did not have any guile in his heart, hence we could deal with it.'

Kadhi took a minute to digest this and asked, 'May I ask what the result of all this effort was?'

Ghritachi replied, 'Next morning, we reached the riverbank and found the sage seated in meditation. We sat in front of him so that he would see us as soon as he opened his eyes. When he finally awoke from the trance, he smiled and told us the reason for his actions.

'During a trip to Brahmalok the Maharishi had heard that the Kaushik and Bhrigu clans would intermingle in the future. Since he himself is the eldest son of Maharishi Bhrigu, he set about testing all the sons of Kush, your grandfather,' she said, turning to Kadhi, 'to assess which of us would be worthy in-laws.'

Kushanabh chuckled as he thought of those days. 'Apparently, he had already tested the patience of my three brothers and had found them wanting! Thankfully, we matched up to his standards and, satisfied with our efforts, he disclosed the true purpose of his visit to us.'

Kadhi was amused at the thought of his uncles and aunts going through the same tests and wasn't surprised at the sage's failed experiment with them. His mood cleared a little and he finally began to understand the grand plan that Rishi Chyavan had set in motion.

'He told us that he was happy and had deemed us worthy to be in-laws to the Bhrigu clan. However, he himself was already married to Sukanya, the daughter of your grand-uncle Shrayati, hence the match would have to wait a generation.'

'That's when I told him about your sisters,' Ghritachi pitched in.

'He told us not to worry and to get your sisters married to Brahmadatt, who had just ascended the throne of Kampilya. Since your brother-in-law is the son of a rishi and a half-nymph, he could match the girls in his genetic make-up.'

Kadhi marvelled at the vast knowledge the rishis possessed as he listened to his mother.

She was saying, 'Our in-laws, Somada and Rishi Chuli, were more than gracious in agreeing to the match. As Kampilya held the hand of each of my girls for the ceremony, they kept getting cured of their disfigurement! What a relief it was to watch them attain their original forms and that was when we realized that the other boon that Rishi Chyavan had bestowed on us would also come true sooner or later.'

'What other boon?' both Kadhi and Satyavati asked together.

Kushanabh smiled at their excitement and replied, 'The boon that we shall be blessed with an incarnation of Indra and that our granddaughter would get married to the rishi's own son when the time was right.'

'It was only on his suggestion that we organized the Putra-kaam-eshti Yagnya to obtain you, Kadhi, from the gods and today, the time has come to fulfil his prophecy regarding our lovely granddaughter.'

Kadhi felt a burden lift off his muscular shoulders. So he did not have to worry about his daughter or his kingdom; destiny had already planned a good future for them.

Kushanabh noticed the change in his body language and patted his head. 'However much importance one gives to free will, in the end, he cannot escape the hand of destiny. In spite of the near impossible condition you have put before Rishi Ruchik, rest assured it shall be met. So cheer up and start preparing for our granddaughter's wedding!'

Adhyaye 5

Ruchik was a worried man.

He had gone to the king to ask for his daughter's hand in marriage because of his father's insistence and had landed up with a new problem instead.

He still could not fathom what he would gain out of a marriage except additional responsibility. He liked to live life on his own terms and did not fancy a woman changing his lifestyle and, if rumours were to be believed, they had a tendency to change a lot of things!

However, he had postponed the Grihasth Ashram for as long as he could and had promised his father that he would finally settle down into the householder's role. He had learnt everything that he could about the girl his father had suggested and, frankly, he hadn't found any excuse to reject her so far. He had even dug into her family's past but again got nothing he could use to turn down this proposal.

Steeling his mind, he had finally gone to the royal court only to be stumped by this almost impossible condition that the king had put before him. The thought had come to him that this could be the perfect way out of an alliance that neither he nor the father of the prospective bride seemed to really want.

Yet, he did not want to accept defeat because of a condition that had clearly been a ploy to dissuade him. If anything, it had only strengthened his resolve to fulfil his mission now that there was a seemingly insurmountable obstacle in front of him.

He was not sufficiently advanced in his spiritual journey as yet to conjure up a thousand steeds of the description that Kadhi had demanded. Nor could he take the help of his father since it was a personal challenge that the king had given him. He would have to find a way to achieve this feat himself.

After some thought, he decided to go to the riverbank to meditate in peace and think of a solution. Travelling on foot, he came across the confluence of the Kalandi and the Ganga and, compelled by the serenity of the place, decided to set base there.

He chose a spot from where he could see the waters of the two rivers mingling and sat down under a great ashwattha tree. The thought of a thousand horses, white like the moon save one black ear, filled his mind. How could he make it come true . . . Surely there was someone who could help him!

He realized he would have to take divine help in order to fulfil this promise. Who was best suited and, more importantly, would be inclined to help him achieve this goal? Would the wind god help him in this endeavour? Maybe not, given his history with the daughters of Kushanabh!

He thought next about invoking Varun, the lord of water; he was rumoured to have a predilection for horses. He remembered a hymn composed by Atri Muni that spoke of him as the provider of strength in steeds and milk in cows. Yes, maybe he should give it a shot but he decided to try to create a steed on his own first.

He thought of the spells he knew and realized that even if

he could not create the huge number of horses that had been demanded, he could perhaps create a prototype on his own and, as the sun began slipping towards the horizon, he started chanting mantras that could conjure up a living, breathing, galloping steed of the colour he had in mind.

As he concentrated harder on achieving his goal, an amorphous shape began to emerge from the foam splashing at the riverbank.

It started coalescing into a ball of water that caught the light of the setting sun and the moonbeams of a rising full moon, absorbing the radiation of both the celestial bodies, imbibing their energies into its heart. All of a sudden, a spark seemed to come to life in its centre. Within minutes the sphere changed form and took the shape of a mare's womb.

To a casual onlooker, it would have been an amazing sight. Within that watery womb, the spark was developing into a foal, an entire solar year of gestation taking place within seconds. The ontogeny would have been astounding to watch since an equine embryo passes through many transitions before it actually starts to resemble a horse.

As soon as the baby was fully developed it let out a neigh of gratitude. The sage opened his eyes and glanced at his creation with satisfaction. It was a beautiful silver foal, with its left ear tipped black and a tiny horn on its head!

Ruchik beamed with pride at the perfection of his creation and raised a hand to bless the newborn, simultaneously chanting a mantra to speed up its development. Within a few moments, there was a full-grown unicorn standing on the riverbank, tossing its head haughtily, showing off its golden mane.

Ruchik felt excited. This was the first time he had tried to create a living being and to succeed in his very first attempt!

His objective achieved, he closed his eyes to pray to Varun to obtain the remaining 999 horses and chanted the very mantra that had come to his mind earlier.

> *I sing forth unto the mighty Varun, who keeps the earth*
> *   apart from the sky.*
> *The provider of life to trees, strength to horses, milk to cows,*
> *   and wisdom to the minds of men.*
> *He laid Fire in water, Soma in the stone and made the two*
> *   worlds wet with Rain.*
> *He clothes the mountains with clouds and makes the*
> *   meadows fertile.*
> *It is only his power that lets rivers pour into the Ocean,*
> *   yet they fill it not.*
> *O Varun, forgive the sins I may have committed to friend,*
> *   comrade or brother;*
> *To family or to the stranger; knowingly or in ignorance.*
> *Forgive my sins, O Varun, and may I be dear to thee*
> *   hereafter.'*

The initial salutations done, he tried creating a mental connection with the lord of the oceans.

He focused on projecting his desire for the horses in the form of mental waves that spread outwards from his mind. After some effort, his thoughts leapt to the river in wave after wave of pure energy that merged with the flowing waters gleaming in the moonlight.

After an hour and a half of telepathic transmission, Ruchik sensed a response emanate from the depths of the river. It began as a faint rumble that steadily grew louder. The two rivers seemed

'{Rig Veda, Book 5, Verse 85}

to be churning in an invisible cauldron and their confluence seemed like a whirlpool. Ruchik felt all this happening around him even though his eyes were closed in a deep trance.

The rumbling was now increasing in amplitude and, seconds later, the first of the 999 horses emerged from the vortex, bathed in the sacred waters of the Ganga. The creature glowed as if it was made of the very moonbeams that reflected off its radiant pelt, and its silver mane flew majestically as it galloped across the water and came to kneel on the bank in a posture that would have been difficult for an ordinary horse to hold for long. Its appearance was followed by that of another and another till the entire riverbank teemed with horses that were the colour of the moon and had one black ear each. As the last of the horses appeared from the waves, Ruchik opened his eyes and surveyed the herd. He did not have to count them for he had known instinctively when the penultimate horse had emerged from the water.

As he stood up, the unicorn turned and knelt before him as the leader of all the assembled horses.

Ruchik couldn't believe that his very first attempt at harnessing his mystical powers had given him such handsome results. As he was counting his blessings, he realized he now had a different problem on his hands: how would he transport all these steeds to Kanyakubja?

He folded his hands and prayed to Varun once again, requesting the lord to give him a solution.

In an instant all the horses disappeared save the unicorn that Ruchik himself had created. Ruchik panicked and looked around. Had Varun taken away the horses, annoyed by his never-ending demands? He closed his eyes and wished for the horses to reappear and, lo and behold, they were there in front of him, neighing and tossing their heads.

The rishi realized that Varun had given him a wonderful solution. The horses could appear whenever and wherever he wished them to.

He fell down on his knees and thanked Varun for coming to his aid, promising to establish a pilgrimage point at this very place. He would make sure that generations to come would remember his generosity and visit this Ashwatirth to bow to the great lord of the oceans.

His mission accomplished, he jumped on to the back of the snow-white unicorn and galloped towards the city of the hunchbacked maidens.

Adhyaye 6

This time Kadhi welcomed him with genuine happiness, a change that Ruchik couldn't help but notice.

In front of the gathered assembly, the rishi proudly declared, 'Rajan, I bring with me a fleet of one thousand horses, each white as the moon save one ear each. I have fulfilled your condition and kept my promise. I hope you are ready to keep your end of the bargain as well.'

Kadhi accepted the rishi's words even though he could not see any of the horses Ruchik spoke of.

He asked in a mild manner, 'I accept your word for the presence of the horses, O learned sage, but it would be good for the assembly here to actually see them, if you don't mind!'

Ruchik understood the king was saying this light-heartedly and wondered what had happened in his absence to cause this positive change. Unaware of his own father's real role in the situation, he merely smiled and nodded in agreement.

Taking a dramatic turn towards the open end of the arena, he clapped his hands twice. Instantly, the lights in the circular hall seemed to turn dim and a fragrant mist filled the hall.

The entire gathering watched in awe as the different phases of moon on the midnight-blue roof seemed to swirl around and coalesce into silver-grey clouds. Even as they gazed at the ceiling in awe, fine flakes of snow started floating from above and the first one landed on Kadhi's shoulder.

The king looked at the falling flakes in disbelief and then turned to glance at Ruchik.

The rishi smiled and gestured towards the entrance. Out of the gathering mist and falling snow, a shape was emerging. A muscular milk-white horse with a flowing golden mane entered the hall at the far end. As it gracefully cantered into the light, the people sitting closest to it let out a gasp and the reason became apparent to the king soon enough.

It wasn't an ordinary horse but a living, breathing unicorn!

The king was impressed and so was the assembly. Till date no one had seen a unicorn on Earth though they had heard rumours of their sightings near the North Pole where Kuber, the lord of riches, resided.

One by one, other horses started appearing, each white as the moonlight save for one ear that was black. Kadhi knew if all of them arrived here the citizens would probably cause a stampede so he urged the rishi with folded hands, 'The entire rajya sabha has witnessed the fulfilment of your promise, my lord. I request you to order the horses to appear in my stables instead of the assembly hall so that they may be taken care of appropriately.'

Ruchik acknowledged his request and clapped his hands again. At once the pattern on the ceiling changed and the mist and snow disappeared. All the horses filed out of the hall in a disciplined manner; only the unicorn remained by the rishi's side.

Kadhi got up from his throne and embraced Ruchik before announcing to the entire hall, 'I hereby declare the terms of my condition fulfilled and vow to give the hand of my daughter Satyavati to Rishi Ruchik in marriage. Let the festivities begin!'

Adhyaye 7

The wedding was a grand affair and the royal families of all neighbouring kingdoms attended the ceremony to bless the newly-weds. Satyavati even got to meet her aunts who, after being cured of their curse, had been living in Kampilya with their husband.

Kadhi had accepted the 999 horses that had originated from the river as a gift from Varun but had let his daughter and son-in-law keep the unicorn along with other gifts. Ruchik accepted the unicorn but graciously returned all other presents that Satyavati's parents wanted to bestow on their daughter. He told them that they would be living in the forest, where there would be no need for all these luxuries.

In the midst of all the events that took place, no one had noticed the quiet change that had come over Satyavati. She had barely spoken since the day Ruchik returned with the horses and had accepted her destiny with an equanimity that belied her age.

It wasn't that she was unhappy, but she could not be completely happy as well. Her dreams of becoming a valiant warrior and a ruler had been shattered by one cruel stroke of fate, yet she was gracious in her behaviour towards Ruchik throughout the ceremony.

Now, as they sat in the ashram, talking for the first time as man and wife, she poured her heart out and berated him for demanding her from her father as if she was an object or an animal. She knew their marriage had been predestined but she wanted to fight against her destiny.

She berated him for bringing misery to her parents who had not harmed any person ever and had only strived to better the lot of their people. Most of all, she cursed him for taking away the dream she had nurtured all her life.

Ruchik listened to her patiently, trying to understand the emotions flowing through her heart.

After she had calmed down, he said, 'Princess, I agree that when I had first arrived at your father's palace, I had not given any thought to what your own dreams would be. I was just following the orders of my father and was too engrossed in my own reluctance to begin a householder's life to pay attention to what my prospective bride may have in her mind.'

Satyavati looked at him, searching for an expression that may give away his lie. In her mind she had already branded him a villain but the honesty in his eyes made her doubt her own preconceived notion.

Ruchik was gracious and apologized profusely while cursing himself for being so self-centred. He took her hand in his and said, 'I cannot undo the past but I can strive to give you a bright future. This is the first day of our life together and I promise to never neglect you for my hermitic duties and to fulfil all your desires to the best of my abilities. You shall be free to visit your parents anytime you want to assist them in looking after their kingdom and my unicorn shall be at your service whenever you wish to ride back home.'

For a moment, Satyavati felt she should test his word and ride the unicorn back to Kanyakubja immediately. But then she realized the sincerity of his tone and her anger gradually subsided. However, she still needed to figure out a way to help her parents, for without an heir even the mightiest of kingdoms eventually crumbled.

Since he was so repentant, she asked for Ruchik's help to balance Mahodayapur's loss of one heir with another.

She said, 'I believe in your words, and appreciate the efforts you are making to make me feel at home. But our marriage has resulted in a vacuum on the throne of my father's kingdom. He is past the prime of his life and needs someone to assist him.'

Ruchik agreed with her and asked what she had in mind.

Satyavati replied, 'I know it would be unfair on my part to ask you to move to the city and live in the palace when you desire to live an ascetic's life. Therefore, I would like us to relinquish all our rights on our firstborn, and hand him or her over to my parents to be crowned as the next heir so that the royal throne of the Chandravanshis does not stay vacant.'

Ruchik looked at his wife with renewed respect and softly said, 'I am honoured to have as my wife a princess so knowledgeable in Dharma that she did not bind me to my words and ask me to move to her home. I am equally impressed by your devotion to your citizens that makes you offer your own child for the welfare of the kingdom! But hear me out, princess, and tell me if you agree with what I say. If our own child became the next ruler of Mahodayapur, wouldn't it entangle us in the politics of the royal court and the infinite entrapments of the material world?'

Sulking, Satyavati looked at him and asked, 'Rishivar, are you taking advantage of my honourable behaviour and refusing to keep your promise?'

Ruchik smiled, shook his head and suggested an alternative. 'I have earned enough mystical powers to twist the hands of fate slightly and I think I have a solution to this dilemma. Why don't I use my powers to bless both you and your mother with sons? That way, the kingdom would get its heir, the royal family would be complete again and both of us could still live our lives in the peace and quiet of the ashram.'

Satyavati marvelled at this idea and said, 'Forgive my incredulity but can you actually do that?'

Ruchik smiled and reminded her of the 999 horses he had obtained from Varun and the unicorn he had created all by himself that still roamed outside the ashram.

Laying a reassuring hand on her shoulder, he said, 'When one inadvertently crushes someone's cherished dream, it becomes one's duty to try and replace it with a better dream. Invite your parents to our humble abode next week so that we can discuss this proposal. I shall try to balance out my earlier thoughtlessness by honouring the dream that you and your parents had shared. You will not regret marrying this sage; I hope to make you the happiest woman in this kingdom.'

Adhyaye 8

It was the first praher of the day and Ruchik had woken up early as per his routine. He would bathe in the river, perform his ablutions and complete his morning prayers as the sun god's chariot rose above the horizon.

All this was according to his usual schedule but later he had a bigger task to accomplish. He had been married to Satyavati for a week now and today was the day her parents would be visiting to check on her welfare.

As he came back from the river, he took a detour and went deeper into the forest, gathering roots and plucking leaves of at least a dozen herbs that enhanced specific traits in a person. Then he picked berries that enhanced the receptivity of a uterus for the embryo. Returning to the hut, he prepared a dish of barley, rice and pulses, adding the berries to the mixture. He then divided the gruel in two bowls and added a different set of herbs to each, mixing them in along with butter and milk.

Thereafter, he put one portion in the shade of an ashwattha tree and the other under a giant fig, blessing both by means of magical incantations. Once all this was done, he woke up his new wife so she could get ready to welcome her parents.

By the second praher they began to hear the distant sounds of an approaching cavalcade. There were the telltale sounds of horses' hooves, elephants' trumpeting and the resultant tumult caused amongst the forest animals.

Within an hour the royal procession had reached their doorsteps. Satyavati had worked hard to line the way to their hut with petals of wild flowers whose heady fragrance lingered in the air. She had made garlands of fresh lotuses to greet her parents with and lemonade to refresh the entire entourage.

As the king and the queen got out of their chariot, the newly-weds bent down to touch their feet.

Kadhi raised Ruchik by his arms and said, 'Thank you, my dear son-in-law, for this pleasant welcome. The cool breeze of your abode suffused with the pleasant aroma of wild flowers fills my heart with a peace I haven't felt in a long time.'

Ruchik accepted Kadhi's gracious words even though he knew the king and the queen were probably used to much grander ceremonies. He thanked his father-in-law and said, 'Rajan, I am humbled by your kind words and again reminded of the goodness of your heart that remains incorruptible even by the luxuries of royal life.'

Satyavati beamed with pride and said, 'That's my father for you! Welcome to our humble abode, father and mother.'

She embraced her mother lovingly and together all four of them made their way to the hut. The king's soldiers and attendants were told to set up camp near the river and the cooks were instructed to prepare a meal worthy of the occasion.

When the pleasantries were over, Ruchik cleared his throat and addressed the three of them, 'I did grave injustice to the kingdom of Mahodayapur by taking away their selected regent. Not only that, I have also broken your hearts by bringing your daughter so far away from your eyes and I apologize for all the hurt that my actions have caused you unknowingly.'

Satyavati's eyes filled with tears on hearing her husband ask for forgiveness with such a clear heart.

Kadhi took a moment to digest what he had heard. 'My dear son-in-law, what you did was written by the hands of destiny. Let us not lament the past and look to the future instead. It fills my heart with pleasure to see my daughter happy in this ashram and I credit both her resilience as well as your gracious behaviour for that. Truly there's no better happiness than getting the right partner in life!' he said, looking at his own wife and smiling.

Queen Ratna came closer to him and held his hand. 'I agree, my dear king,' she said.

'The happiness on our daughter's face is proof enough that our son-in-law is taking good care of her and I thank you, Rishi Ruchik, for the same. Also, we would be honoured if you would not refer to us by our titles and call us father and mother instead.'

Ruchik, not used to such words of high praise, blushed and said, 'Please don't embarrass me. When I took your daughter away, I assumed responsibility for her. She is my better half and it is my duty, nay honour, to look after her happiness. And as proof of my intention, I have decided to utilize whatever powers I have earned through penance to make the gods bless both my wife and the queen mother with sons.'

Kadhi and Ratna were astonished by this declaration. The king got up in surprise. 'My dear son, you fill me with wonder! Because of the complications during Satyavati's birth, the royal vaidyas had declared that Ratna would never be able to conceive again, hence we did not have another child. Is what you say truly possible?'

Ruchik nodded at both the elders and explained, 'What science cannot cure, divine intervention can. I have prepared a potion imbued with mystical powers and the essence of food grains, herbs and berries that can provide an environment suitable for the development of a child. Mother and Satyavati need to partake of the potion and I am certain that they will be able to conceive sons who shall bring great pleasure to both our families.'

Satyavati was not aware that Ruchik had already begun bringing her desire to fruition and rushed to him with tears in her eyes. 'You are truly the best husband I could have dreamt of! I expressed my concern to you only a few days ago and you have already worked out the solution for it.'

Ruchik took her hand in his own and solemnly said, 'A promise should be fulfilled as early as possible, my dear, so that one's mind is free of any burden. I do this not just for our happiness but that of the entire kingdom of Mahodayapur.'

Hearing Ruchik's words, Kadhi and Ratna beamed with pride. They walked to their daughter and son-in-law and hugged them both. After few moments, Ruchik broke away from the huddle and left, promising to join them after his daily meditation.

Before departing, he told Satyavati that the gruel he had prepared was meant to be eaten just before sunset and that she should give the pot under the ashwattha tree to her mother while she herself was to consume the one kept under the fig tree. Saying so, he left for the forest, little knowing that fate doesn't change the plans of just ordinary human beings but also those of rishis of the highest order.

As evening approached, Satyavati and Ratna grew eager to partake of the magical gruel.

They went out to the trees and picked up their respective potions. As they waited for the sun to set a thought came to the queen's mind.

She mulled over it for a while before finally saying, 'Daughter, I have a nagging thought in my mind and wish to share it with you. It is human nature to desire the best for one's own family and it is quite likely that your husband feels the same.'

Satyavati was confused. 'What do you wish to imply, mother?'

The queen clarified, 'Don't get me wrong, I don't doubt for a second that Ruchik has blessed both the potions with his powers but isn't it likely he saved the best for his own child? Would it be too presumptuous to imagine that to be possible?'

Satyavati's brow furrowed in anxiety and she said, 'Do you really think so, mother? From whatever time we have spent together, I find it hard to believe he might be capable of such duplicity!'

Ratna shook her head. 'I do not intend to blame him for any such conscious intent but wouldn't it be natural that subconsciously he may have done as I say? After all, the human mind is fickle and difficult to control, even if you are a gifted rishi.'

Satyavati thought about this and it seemed to make sense to her. 'You may be right, mother. But what should we do? He wanted us to take the potion at the precise hour of sunset; should we wait for him to come back and confirm the same?'

The queen pondered a moment. 'Well, my dear, even if you ask, it is unlikely that he will acknowledge such a situation since he might not be even consciously aware of it. Moreover, his instructions were very clear: we are to consume the gruel at the exact moment the sun goes down.

'Maybe what we should do is exchange our potions in case what we suspect actually happened. If both potions are equally potent, it should make no difference to the original plan, but if they are not . . .' she paused before continuing, 'then the future king of Mahodayapur would stand a better chance. After all we need to think of the bigger picture here—that of the future of our kingdom.'

As Satyavati chewed on this thought, her mother added, 'For me, both children would be dear, one born from my womb and other from my daughter's. But as I see it, the king of Mahodayapur will need more blessings than my grandchild who, in all probability, will spend his life in the forest and follow in the footsteps of his father and become an ascetic.'

The logic seemed to appeal to Satyavati. If worst came to worst, her son would be less talented than her new brother. Would that be such a big issue? After all, her brother would require the special blessings that had eluded their kingdom till now.

She told her mother, 'I agree to what you have suggested, mother. Let us exchange our pots and consume the potion at the right moment. I can discuss what we have done with Ruchik when he comes home.'

Thus decided, the two ladies exchanged their potions and consumed it even as the sun plunged below the horizon.

Shortly after, the royal entourage prepared to leave at dusk. The king could not stay away from his city for a long time and, after waiting for the sage to return from the forest, Kadhi requested Satyavati to give her husband their regards and invited both of them to visit them as soon as they could. Satyavati was sad to see her parents go but her heart beat with excitement, knowing that she would soon be conceiving a new life within her womb.

As she waited for Ruchik to come back home, she lay down on her bed and thought about giving birth to a baby boy who would become the spiritual guide of his brother, the new king. It would be the perfect combination and the boys could become best friends if she could raise them together.

When Ruchik came home, he apologized for missing bidding farewell to the king and queen since he had lost track of time while meditating. He hugged Satyavati and inquired about the potion and she nodded in acknowledgement. In her excitement, though, she neglected to mention the exchange to Ruchik and they lay together as man and wife, allowing for his seed to be firmly planted in her womb by the merit of the potion she had imbibed.

As she drifted into sleep later that night, Satyavati's dream had acquired a different character. The Brahmin boy she had imagined earlier, reading scriptures with his father's concentration and a toothless smile, had been replaced by a boy covered in mud and gore. The book in his hand was replaced with an axe and his face was twisted in a snarl as the rivers of Aryavarta turned red with blood around him.

Adhyaye 9

Ten lunar months had passed and there was celebration in Mahodayapur. The citizens who were once worried about the future of their kingdom were dancing around with joy. Both the queen and the princess had been blessed with handsome baby boys radiant as Chandra Dev himself.

As was the custom, Satyavati had spent the last three months of her pregnancy in her mother's home while Ruchik had moved to the Himalayas for that duration. He had planned his trip in such a way that he would be back in time for the delivery and had, consequently, just returned to the capital this morning.

While the babies were being cuddled and blessed by senior members of the royal household, Ruchik sat with the kulguru to prepare the birth charts of the two babies. The new prince had been named Vishwarath, in anticipation of his conquest of the world aboard his chariot, while the Brahmin infant was named Yamdagni, one who burnt with an inner fire of spiritual quest.

To Ruchik's surprise, there seemed to be a mismatch in both the birth charts and he could not understand the reason for it. The chart of his new brother-in-law should have been showing the traits that his own son's chart was showing. When he checked Yamdagni's chart he found the same anomaly there—it was almost as if the fates of the two boys had been exchanged!

How was that possible? He had clearly told his wife which potion to take and he was sure she would have followed his directions. Or had she?

He closed his eyes and sat down to meditate on the cause. The events of that fateful evening flashed in front of his eyes. As he slowly realized what had happened, his eyes shot open in anger.

What did these infernal women think of themselves! They may be royalty but that did not give them the right to doubt his integrity.

He threw the birth charts on the floor and stormed towards his wife's chamber. For the first time in his life Ruchik felt betrayed and he intended to convey his displeasure to his wife in no uncertain terms. As he barged into her chamber, the maids scampered, seeing his temper. Fortunately, none of their relatives were around and he could talk to her without upsetting anyone else.

Satyavati had been nursing the baby but fear gripped her when she saw Ruchik's face. In a moment of clairvoyance she understood what he was upset about and silently cursed herself for not discussing it with him earlier.

Ruchik had every intention of screaming his lungs out but seeing her spent and exhausted in the bed, holding their child in her arms, momentarily curbed his rage. He knew he would not be able to let his anger out at that moment but, in his mind, a resolve started to take shape.

He walked slowly to the bed and sat down on one corner. 'I know what you and your mother did, princess,' he said in a barely restrained tone, deliberately using the title that she had left behind when she married him.

'How could you doubt my sincerity for even one moment when I was only trying to fulfil your own desire? Your mother thought she could take back the destiny that was stolen from her so she asked you to exchange the gruel without realizing the far-reaching effects your actions would have!'

Satyavati cowered in fear and the newborn started wailing.

Ruchik tried to control his tone and said calmly, 'For whatever it is worth, let me confess that you and your mother were correct in one respect. I did differentiate between the two potions. But do you know the reason?

'I had enhanced the potion I had prepared for you so as to provide our child the perfect qualities of a Brahmin and enable him to become one of the most accomplished sages of our time while your mother's potion was spiked with herbs that promote aggression and valour to make him a fit Kshatriya ruler.'

He paused to take a breath and said, 'Because of your foolishness, our son shall now have a warrior's inclination while your brother shall be born with the inclinations of a Brahmin. Unwittingly, you and the queen have ruined whatever chances your kingdom had of getting a good ruler.'

Satyavati was appalled and fell at her husband's feet. 'Ruchik, please do not utter such inauspicious words! We did this in ignorance and I apologize for doubting you! I beg of you, please tell me how I can atone for this act.'

Seeing the wife he had loved for little less than a year crying and repenting, Ruchik realized how potent the bonds of family could be. He understood why the queen had done what she had and tried to forgive them both in his mind.

He placed his hand on Satyavati's sobbing head and asked her to stop. 'What is done is in the past now. You were magnanimous enough to forgive my selfish act of asking for your hand so I hereby repay your debt by forgiving you for this transgression.'

Satyavati heaved a sigh of relief and folded her hands wordlessly while Ruchik continued, 'I cannot change the future of your brother but this child was borne from my own seed; since you seem so appalled at having a Kshatriya son, I shall modify his destiny so that the trait skips one generation. Now, it shall be your grandson who will be born with those propensities that make you cower in fear.'

While Satyavati absorbed the purport of the words just spoken, Ruchik looked into the eyes of the woman he had loved and had even dared to dream of a long future with. As a result of the incidents that had happened, the resolve taking shape in his mind had further strengthened and he felt even more detached from the world than he had been in the far-off white mountains.

This one episode had proved sufficient to break his faith in all temporary relationships permanently. His grey eyes filled with a steely resolve that Satyavati had never seen before.

'I have decided to permanently move to the Himalayas,' he told her.

He took his eyes away from her face and declared, 'I shall return to my vows of celibacy and spend my life away from this world of infernal lies and fraternal ties. As the child's father, I shall keep an eye on him through my mystic powers and ensure that he never falls in life but that will be the extent of my involvement in raising him.

'At the very outset I was against getting married, yet my father asked me to. So I came to your father and asked for your hand, thus starting a chain reaction that has ultimately made me aware of reality once again.'

Satyavati looked on in mute horror as her entire world seemed to collapse around her. She was frantic and tears fell copiously from her already inflamed eyes. She begged Ruchik to stay and not give in to a rash decision that they might regret later but he was determined.

With one look at his newborn child, Ruchik turned away and stormed out of the room, never to come back into their lives again.

Adhyaye 10

A full moon rose over Kanyakubja, bathing the city in its golden splendour, but its beauty was lost on the grieving king and his family.

It was the night of Guru Purnima and the entire day the royal family had been busy meeting and honouring the various acharyas and rishis residing in their kingdom. Kushanabh had started the annual tradition of honouring learned men on this day and this was the first time Kadhi and Ratna were participating with their son, daughter and grandson.

The boys were hardly a few days old but after Ruchik's showdown, Kadhi wanted them to be blessed by as many sages and magi as he possibly could take them to. Since he was aware of the Brahmin propensity in his own son, he was eager for him to begin military training as soon as he began walking. Finding the right teacher was therefore imperative.

Yamdagni would also require a spiritual guide and Kadhi wanted both the boys to learn from the same teacher if possible so that they developed a camaraderie and could help each other in the future. Of all the rishis he had met throughout the day, there was only one that seemed to fit the bill.

The man in consideration sat outside the palace boundaries, sharing the food given as prasadam with stray dogs on the street. He seemed youthful yet wise for his age. A trident lay beside him and he wore rudraksh beads and saffron robes that were a complete contrast to his milky-white skin.

When Kadhi saw him from a distance, his first thought was that he was disrespecting the sanctified food. He walked up to where the young rishi sat and was about to admonish him when the man looked up. Kadhi was shocked—the man had three eyes!

He immediately understood that this was no ordinary rishi and fell down at his feet.

The young sage looked at him with compassion and said in a voice that boomed like thunder, 'Dear king, don't be apologetic, for even if the words forming in your mind were rough the intention behind them wasn't.'

Kadhi apologized for what he had been about to say.

The rishi laughed and said, 'Why should I feel hurt by your unsaid words? You provided food to a hungry sage who just happened to be passing through your kingdom on his journey to the great white mountains. I should be thankful to you for your kindness, for words dissolve in thin air and dissipate but food dissolves in the gastric juices to provide energy.'

Kadhi realized this man was an accomplished sage and humbly asked him who he was. The young sage revealed his name—Dattatreya.

The king could not believe his ears. This was the Dattatreya whom legend declared to be the incarnation of Lord Shiva himself! The author of *Tripura Rahasya*, a treatise on Advaita Vedanta, and the brother of the moon god to whose lineage the Chandravanshis belonged!

Though he must have been extremely old, his body radiated the youth and charm of an adolescent boy. He seemed to be a younger, fairer version of Lord Shiva himself with his three eyes, matted hair and a trident lying by his side.

Kadhi wondered why such a personage was associating with lowly animals and Dattatreya smiled in response to his thoughts.

'I have an affinity for these creatures and they seem to sense it,' he said. 'Wherever I go I find myself surrounded by them and I love their company. I have learnt one thing in the world of men: A human being may let you down by his/her actions but a dog will always stay by your side no matter what you do or fail to do. These are the most guileless and loving creatures on this planet and I shared the prasadam with them to give them the benefit of its sanctified nature.'

Kadhi saw the deep thought behind the Avatar's actions and decided right then to ask him to become the guru of his princes. In response to his unspoken question, Dattatreya replied, 'Even though my intention while passing through was to reach the abode of my Lord Shiv Shankar, I sense you have a greater need for my presence here.'

Satyavati had been riding a little behind on her unicorn and, as she got closer, she was struck by the appearance of the rishi her father was talking to. She dismounted and bowed.

Kadhi introduced her. 'My lord, this is my daughter Satyavati whom life has dealt an unfair hand. As you rightly guessed, we require an acharya for her son and mine who can take away the shadows of our past and show them the path to a happy future.'

The Avatar looked at them both and said, 'I would like to meet the boys before taking a decision.'

Kadhi immediately summoned a chariot to take Dattatreya to the palace and personally drove him there. He sent Satyavati to ride ahead of the chariot and inform her mother of their arrival.

When they reached the steps of the palace, Kadhi reined in the horses and ran to the back of the chariot to help the Avatar descend. Dattatreya, however, jumped out of the chariot by himself and walked inside with the king.

Queen Ratna was already on the doorstep along with Acharya Dhanu, waiting to greet the Avatar. She held a pooja thali in her hands and was about to apply vermilion on his forehead when she noticed the third eye and let out an involuntary gasp. Dattatreya smiled and in an instant his third eye disappeared. The queen managed to control her reaction and applied tilak above the eye before showering the visitor with marigold petals. The three of them then led the guest into the visitors' chamber while Satyavati made sure the attendants provided everything required for his comfort.

After the formalities were over, Kadhi asked Satyavati to bring the boys for Dattatreya's blessings. As they were brought into the chamber by their respective mothers, the rishi noticed the similarity in their features. Both resembled Kadhi somewhat but Yamdagni had his father's grey eyes and dusky complexion while Vishwarath seemed fairer and had a shock of curly hair like his father. Dattatreya placed his hands on their heads and silently whispered a blessing.

After the boys were sent away with the maids he addressed the royal family, 'Dear king, I see the blessings of Rishi Ruchik on your sons. They both have an inner strength that will hold them in good stead in the years to come. After meeting them, I feel as if it is my Karma to guide them in life and I shall be glad to take them under my tutelage.'

Kadhi heaved a sigh of relief on hearing this.

The rishi added, 'However, both of them have their individual personalities and I shall train them accordingly. Your sons possess great potential for spiritual growth so I'll guide them towards that pursuit.'

The king felt troubled and folded his hands in supplication. 'My lord, you are aware of the benediction of Rishi Ruchik, yet

I request you to not impart to my son any deep teachings from the scriptures. That education can be shared with Yamdagni who can guide Vishwarath later in life.

'I would request you to train Vishwarath exclusively in the use of astras and shastras and make him adept in the art of war, and teach him about good governance for I do not want to turn him into a dictator with only the knowledge of his power to guide him. My grandson should be trained to become his spiritual guide and mentor later in life.'

Dattatreya seemed to consider the request. 'My king, I understand the trepidation in your mind and I agree under the circumstances perhaps it may be best to refrain from sharing the knowledge of our scriptures with the boy. Yamdagni will of course receive the ancient knowledge I possess and can more than make up for Vishwarath's ignorance in these matters.'

Satyavati and Ratna could not believe their good fortune! Even after the miscalculation that had led them to commit an error of such proportions, the future seemed to be turning out fine for both the boys. Together the family knelt before the Avatar and bowed low in reverence.

The rishi blessed them individually. 'Kadhi, you have been a good king and your reign has been most prosperous for the kingdom of Mahodayapur. You have not transgressed against any of your neighbours and have only annexed a kingdom when a tyrant was brutally subjugating his citizens. Leave your worries behind; the worst phase of your life is over and the future holds only contentment.'

Kadhi touched the feet of the Avatar who smiled and put his hand on the king's head. The sage then called the queen forward, and placed his hand on her head as she knelt before him. 'Queen Ratna, you have been instrumental in keeping Kadhi's personal as well as professional lives in balance and you are indeed the Lakshmi of this kingdom.

'You have committed an error in judgement because of which you suffer mental anguish now but, rest assured, the results of that act will not jeopardize the future of your children. If anything, it will only draw the inevitable closer and bring great fame to your clan. Do not feel guilty any more and let go of your trauma.'

Dattatreya's words calmed the inner storm that had tormented Ratna since the day Ruchik had left her daughter. Even though Satyavati had taken the blame completely on herself, she could never forget that it was her suggestion that had resulted in their separation. The Avatar's words soothed her mind and gave her the peace she had been missing.

The rishi then asked Satyavati to step forward. Satyavati felt a lump form in her throat and tears gathered in her eyes.

The rishi noticed her pain and blessed her, saying, 'Dear daughter, you have experienced events that can be difficult for the strongest of persons to bear. Destiny has thrown its cards in what may seem an unreasonable manner but believe me when I tell you that the worst is over. Your child is destined to reach the highest spiritual platform while your brother will grow into a brilliant strategist and king who, if sufficiently motivated, could even become a universal monarch.'

Hearing this, Satyavati completely broke down. The guilt of betraying the husband who had doted on her every wish had been killing her but the blessings of the rishi eased her sorrow and the pain flowed out through her tears.

Dattatreya smiled and said, 'I know you worry about the future since the Kshatriya trait predicted by Ruchik will only skip a generation. But rest assured that your grandchild will be no less than an avatar of Shri Hari Vishnu, the Supreme Lord of all living beings. And rejoice in the knowledge that this will have been made possible precisely because of the exchange you and the queen performed.'

Satyavati was suddenly reminded of the story about Jahnu and Ganga she had heard not so long ago from her father. It seemed to her that, unwittingly, she and her mother had also altered the course of history and may have been instrumental in bringing about the birth of another avatar in this world.

Kadhi saw the relief on his wife's and daughter's faces and breathed a sigh of relief himself. It seemed to him that the desires of a lifetime were coming to fruition today.

Vishwarath

Adhyaye 11

The ashram was situated in the foothills of the great white mountains, the abode of Dattatreya's spiritual guide and master, on the northernmost borders of Mahodayapur. It was a lush green valley full of apple and cherry trees, surrounded by towering snow-capped peaks that touched the skies.

As soon as the few villagers residing in the valley had come to know of his presence, they had started flocking for the Avatar's blessings.

Dattatreya had patiently spoken to each of them and stressed the need to give him privacy to continue with his meditation. They had willingly agreed and even helped build a hermitage for him to reside and teach in. The guru, however, did not take any full-time students and concentrated his attention on the royal pupils who had joined him when they were five years old; they were almost eighteen now.

Before moving to the ashram, the boys had been living a life of luxury cocooned in the protection of their kingdom, hence their first journey to the Himalayas, had been an exciting experience. Kadhi had himself come to drop them to the hermitage, beseeching the guru to keep his earlier request in mind. The boys looked more like brothers than uncle and nephew but the differences in their personalities were clearly visible. Vishwarath's demeanour conveyed his position as the heir to the kingdom while Yamdagni seemed more humble and amiable.

After the initial excitement of travelling to a new place had faded, both boys had become severely homesick and pleaded with their guru to take them back to the palace. Vishwarath had been thoroughly pampered by the palace staff hence his discomfort had been greater, but the Avatar managed to calm their anxiety by giving them a glimpse of their respective futures. That had been enough to focus their minds and Dattatreya knew he would not face any more trouble in managing them.

As expected, both of them turned out to be more inclined towards spiritual pursuits rather than military ones and he knew it was the effect of Rishi Ruchik's benediction. But since he had promised Kadhi, for the past twelve years Dattatreya had been giving the king-in-waiting the best military and governance training, simultaneously moulding Yamdagni into a master of philosophy and metaphysics.

Because of his rigorous physical and mental conditioning, Vishwarath's body was chiselled to perfection and his chest was as wide as the barrels of wine that his grandfather loved to indulge in. With limbs as thick as tree trunks, he stood well above even the tallest ashram bull, yet retained a childlike innocence on his face with its high forehead and unruly curls reminiscent of his father.

Yamdagni on the other hand had become more quiet and introspective and sported a lean and fit body. His long hair was tied in a bun on top of his head and he wore the signs of Shiva on his forehead and arms. His face radiated an inner strength that made him look older than his age and his steel-grey eyes were filled with a cool detachment from the world. The years of training in solitude had only brought them closer to each other and Dattatreya knew they would perfectly complement each other.

This winter morning had begun with the appearance of a bright and cheery sun that had unexpectedly turned the weather pleasant. When he sensed his disciples approaching his hut, ready for the day's session, Dattatreya finished his morning meditation and got ready to receive them.

As they greeted their guru and took their usual places, Dattatreya surprised them by saying, 'Boys, today is the culmination of twelve years of our hard work. I have imparted to you all the knowledge I had received from my father, Atri, and mother, Anusuya, and I am left with nothing more to teach you.'

Vishwarath and Yamdagni were surprised at the announcement and looked at each other in bewilderment.

Dattatreya gave them a reassuring smile. 'Don't look worried. I had purposely not informed you of this earlier so as not to distract you from your training. Now that the goals I had set for both of you have been attained to my satisfaction, I can safely declare your education complete.'

His students still sat dumbfounded, looking at his face blankly. Till this moment they had had no idea that their stay in these idyllic surroundings was coming to an end and that they would be returning to their families soon!

Dattatreya continued, 'I am proud of the progress both of you have made in your respective fields and also relieved now that my part in your lives is over and I can proceed towards the next goal of my life. However, I have one last task for you to perform before I give you my blessings and send you back to Kanyakubja.'

Yamdagni cleared his throat and took permission to speak. When Dattatreya nodded he spoke in his deep baritone, 'Gurudev, this announcement has caught us unawares and filled our hearts with mixed emotions. We can't thank you enough for transforming us from spoilt brats into able soldiers of Dharma. It shall be our honour to fulfil whatever task you have in mind for us.'

Vishwarath nodded in assent.

'Very well then!' Dattatreya said. 'Your last task is more of a mental exercise than a physical one. You have to answer a question I ask and you have to think of the solutions separately. Your answers should reflect your understanding of all that I have taught you in all these years and I expect you to give suitable logic to support them. Does that seem fine to you?'

Dattatreya looked at them with raised eyebrows and both nodded in agreement.

Pausing to collect his thoughts, Dattatreya put the question in front of them. 'Listen to the situation I am presenting very carefully. There was once a kingdom in Kumarikandam that prided itself on its military prowess. After a while, it became difficult for the king to keep his highly enthusiastic army occupied since they had defeated most of their enemies and there were only so many wars they could fight.'

He glanced at his pupils to see if they were following him and Vishwarath, ever impatient, said, 'The king should have involved them in sports! That would have channelled their aggression and kept their minds occupied.'

Dattareya smiled and nodded in agreement. 'Thank you for your esteemed advice, Samrat Vishwarath, that is indeed what this particular king did,' he said.

Vishwarath gave a sheepish grin and looked at Yamdagni who smiled at his exuberance and gestured to him to stay calm.

Dattatreya resumed 'Now, it so happened that the king of the neighbouring kingdom was also an avid sportsman and, though he was of a peaceful nature, had nurtured his army in a similar manner. The two kings were on friendly terms and one day hit upon a plan to organize a contest between their two teams.'

'However, the night before the contest, both kings had a strange dream. Yamraj, the lord of death, was standing by their beds, warning them that the son of the king of whichever team won on the morrow would die!'

His pupils were riveted by the tale and the Avatar continued, 'And the dream did not end there. As soon as Yamraj left, the goddess of wealth, Lakshmi, appeared. She told them that the kingdom to which the losing team belonged would lose all its riches forever.

'Since they had agreed to the contest, the kings could not go back on their word and cancel the event, which meant that at the end of the day there would be a winner and a loser. The two kings now had a duty to win the match for the welfare and prosperity of their subjects even though the kingdom that won would also end up losing its heir.'

Vishwarath and Yamdagni were excited by the moral dilemma the kings were getting into and their guru asked, 'On one side, there is the loss of a son, and on the other, there is injustice to your citizens. Which option should they choose?'

Not surprisingly, Vishwarath was the one to speak first. 'Gurudev, does it befit a king to pay so much attention to a dream? After all, a man's actions make him what he is, not his thoughts. They can't stop living their lives just because of a dream.'

Dattatreya countered, 'You are right that it is a man's Karma which decides his future. But do not forget, it is his thoughts that compel a man to perform the actions. For the sake of this argument let us assume the dreams will come true. Now tell me what you would have done in that condition.'

The princes pondered while the Avatar smiled and sat patiently waiting for their answers. There was no right answer for such a problem but the logic they both used would tell him about their thought process and he hoped it would be in accordance with their future positions in life.

After some moments he asked Yamdagni, 'What do you have to say about this situation, Yama?'

The Brahmin prince was slow to share his opinion but said clearly, 'Gurudev, to me the choice is clear. I believe a king's duty is greater towards his subjects than his own children. So leaving aside the thought of his son he should do what is right for the people.'

Dattatreya nodded his head in acceptance. Yes, Yama would be the perfect guide for Vishwarath's kingdom. He now looked at his other pupil who had been analysing the conundrum from every angle.

Vishwarath cleared his throat and said in his boyish voice, 'I agree with my brother that a king's first duty is towards his subjects but losing a son cannot be an easy thing for a father. It is the duty of a father to protect the life of the offspring he has brought into this world. So if I was in his place, I would put the issue for discussion amongst my people and let them decide. If they cared as much for me as I do for them, they would make a fair choice and we would all work together and rebuild the city!'

Dattatreya was impressed with the conviction as well as the substance of the answer. He knew now the king-in-waiting was on the right path since he had taken the problem to the people and involved them in the decision-making process. That was the hallmark of a true leader.

He gave them the broadest smile they had ever seen and when he spoke his usual grave voice seemed to have a hint of laughter in it. 'My dear students, you do me proud with your answers and your reasoning. Now I am doubly sure that each of you is ready to enter the world of your parents and reclaim your positions.'

Both the boys beamed with pleasure and Yama spoke, 'We are honoured by your words of praise, Gurudev, but would like to ask you that out of the two answers we gave, which one would you have chosen.'

The Avatar gave a deep throaty laugh and shook his head with pleasure.

He then looked at them and said, 'There is no correct answer to situations like this and each of you will have to face the world according to what you deem is the best course of action. However, since you have asked my opinion, I will share with you what I would do.'

The two boys looked at him expectantly and Dattatreya said in a sober tone, 'I would first discuss the matter with the other king and the team captains to make them aware of the situation. Then I would suggest a change in captainship—my team's captain should lead the other team and their captain should lead mine. That way, both captains would still be playing to win but for the other kingdom.

'Thus, we both keep the probability of winning without the fear of losing our sons. Eventually, one team would lose the game but save an heir while the other would win but lose its prince, yet it would not be for want of trying.'

The boys were stumped by the ingenuity of the scheme and looked at their guru in reverence. They realized that they would require a lifetime of experience to come up with ingenuous solutions to such tricky problems and bowed to him in unison.

Dattatreya stood up from his platform and placed his hands on their heads in blessing.

'Yes, my dear children,' he said, 'it does take a lifetime of experience to be able to find a way that is beneficial to a majority for someone will end up losing no matter what you do. I am sure both of you will eventually reach that stage as well but for now, get up and pack up your bags, for the time has come for you to begin the journey back home.'

As the pupils rushed into their huts to pack whatever little belongings they had accumulated over the years, Dattatreya asked the villagers to arrange for their journey back home. Remembering the past twelve years, he thought, no one can escape his Karma. Not even for the sake of fulfilling a spiritual ambition. One could become a true renunciate only after discharging all one's responsibilities towards this world.

Adhyaye 12

Mahodayapur celebrated the arrival of its princes with huge fanfare.

When the princes reached the gates of the capital aboard the simple chariots they were riding, they were welcomed by the governing council and shifted to royal carriages. The king and the queen and Satyavati had personally come to welcome their boys and the family rejoiced in being together after more than a decade.

Though Satyavati and Ratna had visited the boys thrice in this interval, it had been just for a day each time since Dattatreya was very strict about the breaks in his students' training. The king himself had met them but four times and that too during his scheduled tours of the kingdom, so the elders were happy that their children were back where they belonged.

Kadhi and Ratna were delighted to see that the slightly plump, spoilt brat they had raised had turned into a handsome warrior with a fine body and a sharp mind. Vishwarath was witty, charming and full of ambition and they realized that the Avatar had fulfilled his promise quite diligently.

Satyavati couldn't control her tears as she saw in Yamdagni a replica of her husband and realized that her son was all she had left of Ruchik now. Due to Ruchik's blessings, her brother would become a fine king and his son would be the next kulguru and she silently thanked both her husband and Dattatreya for the blessings they had bestowed on the two princes.

The boys were happy to be home and spent the first few days basking in the love and affection of their family, though they realized that even with all this luxury at their disposal they would perhaps never be the same brats they once were. Their guru had changed not only their external forms but also caused a transformation within their hearts.

As they settled into the routine of palace life, Kadhi decided to discuss his future plans with the boys.

He called them to his chamber and said, 'My dear sons, I can't tell you how long I have waited for this day! For the past twenty years I have spent each moment of my life waiting to be released from my responsibilities and I can't wait a minute more to put the burden on your shoulders now.'

Vishwarath understood the import of his father's words and said respectfully, 'It would be an honour for me to relieve you of your burden, father, since I know that this moment has come after a long wait for both you and our kingdom.'

Kadhi nodded and said, 'Your mother and I both agree that the time is right for me to step down and offer the throne to you while Yamdagni serves Mahodayapur in his new capacity as advisor to the king. Both of us and your sister will of course be here to guide you for a few years before we renounce the world and move to the forest.'

The boys bowed down in respect and touched the feet of the king who addressed each of them separately now.

He hugged his son with pride and said, 'Remember, kingship does not imply lordship over your subjects, rather, it implies hard work and tough decision-making, sometimes even at the cost of your personal happiness. I am a lucky father that my son is taking over my responsibilities willingly and with Yamdagni there to guide your path, I have nothing to worry about!'

He hugged his grandson next and told him, 'People are more devoted to their grandchildren than their own offspring and I feel the same love for you. Your mother has endured great sacrifices to see you reach this position and I am proud that you have become a wise Dharmagyata. May your knowledge of Dharma guide this kingdom into prosperity and lead you to spiritual fulfilment.

'Your position is even more important, my boy, than that of the king. For a king might make an error of judgement but his advisors can't afford to be wrong ever,' he finished with a smile.

The princes were then asked to meet their mothers and take their blessings and prepare for the coronation.

For the ceremony that was scheduled the next day, Yamdagni retained his simple attire from all the years of learning under his guru, Dattatreya, but Vishwarath decided to move into his new role with full fanfare. He wrapped an angavastra of green tussar silk, brought by traders from the eastern corners of Himalayas, on his upper body and matched it with a beige dhoti of the finest cotton from the western coast of Nabhivarsh, trying them on for effect.

His curly hair had been teased till it fell in ringlets and he exuded a masculine fragrance of pine and musk. His neck and wrists were adorned with lapis lazuli beads brought especially from Gandhar and he wore rings set with precious stones recovered from the bowels of the southern mines.

Yamdagni took in all the finery and grinned, 'So, Uncle Vishwa, you seem all set to take on the weight of the onyx elephant on your shoulders. I hope the jewels on your fingers and arms do not feel tiny compared to that towering hulk of a throne!'

Vishwarath laughed at the clever reference to the royal throne and said, 'Your dark humour amuses me always, dear nephew. But remember, running a kingdom requires as much showmanship as real capabilities and I am just dressing up for the part,' he ended with a wink.

Yamdagni gave him a playful jab and they both settled down on the soft cushions of his bed.

'Say, brother,' he said, still in jest, 'don't you feel a little nervous at the prospect of running an entire kingdom? Won't the day-to-day decision-making, wars with enemies, internal rebellion, welfare of citizens and keeping a track of palace gossip be difficult to handle? I mean, I will be there to guide and advise you but it's still going to be a tough job.'

Vishwarath smiled at the last sentence and looked at Yamdagni with affection. 'My dear nephew, you are the closest thing to a brother and friend I have had in all these years of training. You know my heart almost as well or perhaps even better than I know it myself! I am raring to go ahead with this and want to don the mantle as soon as father can part with it! Tell me honestly, how do you think I will fare as the king of Mahodayapur?' he asked.

Yamdagni became sombre and replied, 'I have no doubt whatsoever that you will prove to be a really capable king for this kingdom and Mahodayapur will go from strength to strength under your leadership. As long as the strong ambitions that fuel your mind do not take over your logical, thinking brain, I do not envisage any problem in the near future.'

Vishwarath looked at the face of his only close comrade and saw the sincerity in his eyes. He knew what Yamdagni was saying was true, for inside him there was a deep longing to prove himself worthy to the entire world and, if given a chance, he would not rest till he had become the universal monarch.

However, he shrugged off the thought for now and said light-heartedly, 'Well, I don't know about other kingdoms but I will definitely not let my ambition for the ladies take a backseat!' and squinted at the female guards posted in his mother's garden.

Yamdagni guffawed and threw a pillow at Vishwarath before they both ended up rolling in a mock fight. Their eyes were full of dreams and they both hoped reality would be as beautiful as they had imagined all these years.

Adhyaye 13

The years immediately after the coronation went by smoothly.

Vishwarath ruled for a year under the guidance of his father after which Kadhi felt confident enough to leave the throne in his hands. Before retiring to the forest with his queen, he arranged for the princes to get married in ways that would consolidate the empire.

Accordingly, the new king of Mahodayapur was now married to Shalavati, the princess of Kashi; Renumati, the princess of Magadh; and Drishadvati, the princess of Matsya desh. Yamdagni did not have any such strategic obligations to fulfil, hence married once and set up home with his wife Renuka, the princess of Konkan.

Kushanabh and Ghritachi also renounced the material world soon after the wedding, making Satyavati the senior-most member of the royal family.

For a while, the transition seemed to be smooth with only the mantle of ownership changing from Kadhi to his son. Soon, however, Vishwarath's ambition began to surface.

In his first address to the governing council after his father's departure, he looked at each of the council members with a warm smile and said, 'Dear friends and assembled dignitaries, let me first thank you for the immense help I have received from each of you in managing the affairs of our kingdom in recent years. There aren't enough words in any language I know by which I could convey my gratitude to you for making this transition so smooth with your support.'

Then he changed his tone and declared, 'However, I am no longer content with the peace that exists in our nation for I believe we have reached the zenith of our organic growth.'

A murmur broke out amidst the councillors as they wondered what the king really meant by such a declaration. Vishwarath raised a hand, gesturing at them to be quiet. Then he looked into their eyes and said boldly, 'To prosper further, Mahodayapur needs to conquer new lands—that is where the growth of our kingdom lies. It is time to change the status quo.'

Satyavati and Yamdagni looked at each other and sighed. They had known this was inevitable for the years of training that had made Vishwarath a fierce warrior had not been utilized to their full potential since Mahodayapur had peaceful relations with all its neighbours.

Yamdagni said, 'Maharaj, wouldn't it be prudent for the council to discuss the issue before taking a final decision?'

Vishwarath did not mind the question since it was Yamdagni's job as the prime advisor to make sure such big decisions were thoroughly thrashed out in a debate before implementation.

He replied with a determined look directed at the entire council, 'I agree by protocol we should go through a discussion but I have been debating this with myself every single day for a while now. And I assure you, when I put my considerations in front of the council you will all agree as well.'

Some of the senior ministers looked doubtful but Vishwarath knew he could convince them with his logic. This was his first challenge as a king—to make sure his council was in complete agreement with him—and he was determined to achieve the desired result even if it took all his powers of persuasion.

Aloud he said, 'Mahodayapur has an abundance of resources that were garnered in my father's time. In the past couple of years, I have consolidated each aspect of administration, agriculture and trade, trying to maximize the revenue generation and the productivity of our citizens.

'None of us can deny the strides we have taken in terms of improving the health of our people, creating job opportunities and focusing on infrastructure development even in the far-off mountain regions. Our schools are full, talent is in plenty and jobs are sufficient . . . for the time being.'

Here he paused dramatically. 'All is well right now but what happens when our population grows? Because of our excellent doctors, the infant mortality rates have fallen considerably while more and more people are living longer lives. While these developments are praiseworthy, they are also adding numbers to our population at both the age extremes. We need to think about how to keep the elders engaged and to create newer opportunities for the children being born in the kingdom.'

He knew he was making sense and the council would have to agree with his argument even if it did not like it.

An elder member broke the ponderous silence and asked, 'Is war the only way to augment our national income and provide work to the burgeoning population? Mahodayapur has never fought wars for expansion and only defended itself and its neighbours from other belligerent kings. Can't we think of a more innovative way to optimize our resources?'

Vishwarath recognized the elder as his father's oldest supporter. He realized he would have to change the old guard soon if he wanted the council to go along with his decisions.

He shook his head vehemently and said, 'Believe me, uncle, I have considered all possible options and nothing seems to serve the purpose as best as this one. Do not forget that my great-grandfather had done the same when he asked his sons to expand the boundaries of the kingdom instead of dividing it into four parts.'

The elder fell silent but Vishwarath could see other members being swayed by his argument so he further pushed his point. 'At periodic intervals, a kingdom needs to expand its boundaries and establish its dominion for if we do not do it, one of our neighbours might come knocking at our doors with the same ambition. I wish to provide a kingdom large enough for my sons instead of making them toil for it like Grandfather Kush had done.

'Our society is fast reaching a stage where if new elements are not added, it will start stagnating. There is a growing youth population whose aggression needs to be channelled for the benefit of our kingdom. Before trying to convince you further, I would appreciate it if other members in the council also shared their frank opinions.'

Vishwarath knew his logic would appeal to the defence minister so he turned to him first and the minister did not disappoint him.

Clearing his throat, he said, 'It would be good for the troops to get some action since we have been keeping them occupied solely through military exercises for many years now. Mahodayapur has not faced a threat in a long time and we do not know how our troops would fare if one materialized in the future.'

He let his words sink in and then said, 'I agree with the king's suggestion. We could start with a small kingdom to test our army's preparedness and then decide the further course of action.'

Vishwarath felt elated but did not let the relief show on his face. He turned to others now to gauge their reactions.

The minister for human resources said, 'It is true that our young blood is turning lethargic and complacent. While the previous generations toiled and earned their way to comfort, this generation has been born into plenty and does not value what it has.'

Vishwarath was thankful to the minister since he knew every generation considered the next one more pampered and less industrious. Few elders could disagree with this notion so he felt hopeful of getting more support for his campaign.

The youth minister, who paradoxically was an old lady who had been a prodigy in his father's time, said, 'I agree with what you say—war seems like just the right thing to infuse new vigour and build a feeling of patriotism in the youth. However, I cannot support the loss of young lives that a war would entail, for then we would not have any youth left to build the future!'

Vishwarath did not want the argument to turn in the direction of loss so he hastily countered, 'Madam, you seem to place very little faith in our military leadership! With such fine generals as the defence minister here, how could you even entertain the notion of loss of life at our end?'

His words had piqued the defence minister's ego and the old hawk replied hotly, 'There will be minimal loss of life for our soldiers should we go to war. That much I can assure you. We may not have fought in a long time but our preparedness for war is still more adequate than the neighbouring kingdoms'. Plus, a step-by-step approach as I had suggested before will help us decide where to focus and we can rapidly modify the training as required.'

Vishwarath turned to the industries minister, another veteran who seemed to have no opinion whatsoever and was observing the proceedings dolefully. He raised his voice and addressed the septuagenarian, 'A war can kick-start our weapons and logistics industries, spur agricultural growth and give a big boost to invention. Don't you see? This is the opportunity Mahodayapur has been preparing for all its life! The abundant reserves we have, of both food and riches, are the resources that can sustain this campaign and we have never been in a better position to wage such a war.'

The finance minister nodded. 'I agree. It would definitely give a fillip to a lot of industries and put new checks and balances in place. Of course whatever expenditure is incurred on such an exercise would have to be more than compensated for by the returns from the conquered kingdoms.'

Vishwarath looked at the minister who had spoken last and smiled inwardly. The rest of the assembly seemed to be considering these new inputs. He knew the council would never have agreed to his proposal had he only spoken about his own sense of achievement. But, use the right words and everything falls into place.

Besides, what he had said wasn't wrong. Their kingdom did need a new initiative to take it to the next level and he had only presented the true scenario in front of the council.

The fact that it happened to resonate with his personal ambitions was a happy coincidence and, yes, quite convenient as well.

Adhyaye 14

Following the agreement of the council, Mahodayapur launched an aggressive military campaign to expand its frontiers.

Vishwarath's first targets were the smaller kingdoms that had been the protectorates of their relatives' kingdoms and these were won easily. He then moved on to the sister kingdoms of Kausambi, Dharmaranya and Girivraj that had been founded by his grandfather's brothers.

Even though the three kingdoms existed peacefully, Vishwarath wanted them to bow down to his might. His military prowess was unmatched and he showed his mettle riding on his sister's unicorn, shattering limbs and splattering marrow all over battlefields. One by one the three kingdoms fell and Vishwarath established his dominion over them.

It had been a big victory and he decided to sit on it for a while. Any future conquests would require regrouping his new generals and strengthening his army further. Accordingly, he decided to return to Kanyakubja after disbanding the local armies and rewarding the old generals by making them his representatives in the newly won kingdoms.

As he turned his troops back towards his capital, he felt a sense of jubilation and achievement. The world seemed to be in his hands and he could see himself becoming the next Chakravarti Samrat. Little did he realize that life has a way of turning things upside down and changing the proverbial lock just when it seems you have figured out the key to it.

Crossing the mountains of the north where he had studied under his guru, Rishi Dattatreya, Vishwarath sent a major portion of his army ahead and kept a few hundred soldiers behind. He wanted to spend some time roaming through the pine forests and reliving the nostalgia of his youth.

As he passed through the fragrant woods on the northern boundary of his kingdom, he stumbled upon an astonishing sight—right ahead, in a tiny clearing, a snake and a mongoose were basking in the sun, oblivious to each other's presence.

Not very far from them a herd of spotted deer nonchalantly chewed on the lush green grass while a snow leopard stretched out amongst them. The lack of fear in the deer and the absence of aggression in the leopard amazed Vishwarath, as did the apparent indifference of the otherwise sworn enemies—the snake and the mongoose.

This place seemed magical and he decided to explore it on foot. He motioned his soldiers to stay silent and cautiously moved towards the deer. While his movement made the snake slither out of his sight and the deer and mongoose scatter, the big white beast still rolled around in the sun, stretching its back like a domestic cat.

Perhaps, he surmised, these animals have not encountered humans as predators yet. As he moved closer, the big cat took a turn and followed his movements with its keen eyes but still made no attempt to get up or attack. Vishwarath had learnt hand-to-hand combat and could take care of most wild animals with just his dagger but he did not feel threatened at all so let it stay sheathed.

As he came within touching distance, the leopard got up with a swift movement and sat upright, swishing its tail. It let out a soft roar that stopped Vishwarath in his tracks. He pulled out his dagger from its sheath and got ready to defend himself in case the beast attacked.

Within moments, two saffron-robed boys with shaved heads came running towards the leopard. Vishwarath watched in amazement as the two boys petted the big beast and then turned to him.

The older boy addressed him with folded hands, 'O Kshatriya, it is my responsibility to inform you that you are entering the boundary of Brahmarishi Vasishth's hermitage and that no weapons are allowed in this protected sanctuary where humans and all other forms of life live in harmony. May I request you and your men to not use your weapons in this sacred space?'

The king admired the confidence in the boy's voice. He realized that he was not trying to mock Vishwarath's authority since he clearly did not know his true identity. Nodding, he put the dagger back in its sheath.

So this is where the Brahmarishi resides, Vishwarath thought. Now he understood why the creatures of this jungle did not follow the law of the jungle. Vasishth was not an ordinary human but the son of Brahma himself! It wouldn't hurt to take his blessings for the next phase of expansion he had in mind.

Aloud he said, 'Boy, go and inform the Brahmarishi that the king of this land has come to his doorstep and requests an audience with him. My men shall take care not to hurt any creature in this sanctuary.'

The boys immediately ran back to a thatched structure, taking the leopard with them. Soon, an athletic man in his early twenties, with flowing dark hair and a short beard framing his handsome features, appeared. He walked to the king and welcomed him with folded hands and a genuine smile.

'I am Shaktri, the eldest son of Brahmarishi Vasishth and Mother Arundhati. It is an honour for me to welcome our liege to this sacred grove on behalf of my parents and the rest of the ashram,' he said. 'I invite you and your men to refresh yourselves in the waters of the nearby brook. My father shall be waiting to meet you once you feel more comfortable.'

Vishwarath nodded at the young rishi and thanked him for the welcome. He ordered his men to set up camp in the woods and refresh themselves in the brook. He knew how important cleanliness was to these hermits so he himself did the same and then ambled towards the ashram.

As he came closer, his mind was put at ease by the cool breeze flowing from the south. The air echoed with chants from the Vedas and he saw sages of various age groups around the ashram going about their daily routine.

There was a thick aroma of wild rose in the air and the trees were filled with chirping birds of various hues. As he walked closer to what seemed to be the central hut, he saw a rishi of impressive size emerge from the doorway followed by a kindly looking woman who he assumed was the rishi's wife.

They were Vasishth and Arundhati.

The Brahmarishi must have been quite advanced in age, yet looked to be not older than forty. He stood as tall as Vishwarath himself, with a straight back and a well-built frame. His long snow-white hair was kept in place by a string of rudraksh sported by Shiva worshippers; another one adorned his neck. His eyes were the colour of molten lava and the ruddy glow on his cheeks reflected his good health and the effect of continuous living at this high altitude. He wore the saffron garments of an ascetic and the telltale marks of a Vaishnav on his forehead, neck and arms as a sign of his devotion to Lord Vishnu.

Vishwarath knew this was not an ordinary rishi and knelt in front of him with folded hands. 'O learned sage, please accept my humble salutations. It is my good fortune that I can receive your blessings at this stage of my life and request prosperity and abundance for my kingdom.'

The patriarch placed his hand on the king's head and asked him to get up, 'Utishht, Maharaj. This is the first time I am meeting you but I can already sense the great achievements in your recent past. It is the honour of this ashram to welcome you and your men and offer you our hospitality.'

Vishwarath bowed his head and rose. Vasishth then took him to a short wooden rest where they could sit more comfortably. He inquired about the welfare of the royal family and spoke about Rishi Dattatreya.

After chatting for a while Vishwarath decided to take leave but the Brahmarishi invited him to stay for lunch. The king smiled at the naiveté of the hermit and said, 'I thank you, Brahmarishi, for your kind invitation but I have over three hundred men and an almost equal number of animals with me. I hardly think it possible to make arrangements for all of them here!'

Vasishth turned to look at his wife and they both exchanged a smile.

'Don't worry, my king,' he said. 'With the benediction of Shakra, the current Indra, we have the capacity to fill the stomachs of every man, animal or bird that arrives at our door hungry. Six Indras have come and gone in the previous eras, yet I have never seen anyone as generous as him don the mantle of Indra. Please, we request you and all your men to join us for lunch.'

Vishwarath still looked around doubtfully and wondered how it would be possible to feed so many mouths.

Yet, he had heard of the magical powers that rishis possessed so he shrugged and said, 'All right, Brahmarishi. I shall be really interested in observing how this remarkable feat is going to materialize.'

Adhyaye 15

As his men sat down cross-legged amid the towering pine trees, Vishwarath again admired the sylvan surroundings and remembered the old days spent in his guru's hermitage.

Sunlight barely managed to filter through the thick branches and the grass was littered with bursting pine cones. He remembered numerous treks taken with Yamdagni on such slopes when they were at the ashram. Guru Dattatreya had told them that climbing was the best exercise and had made sure they undertook at least one trek or rock-climbing session every day.

Small tables were placed in front of each soldier while Vishwarath himself sat beside the Brahmarishi and his wife and watched in amazement as hermits of the ashram began distributing food amongst his men, filling the leaf plates with rice, lentils, bread, fruit and yoghurt.

He knew his men were as hungry as he was but they waited for their king's order to begin the meal. When the last soldier had been served the assorted food items, Vishwarath gave his men permission to begin. That was just as well since the ravishing aroma of the pure organic food was driving them crazy and his men dug into the sumptuous meal with gusto.

Vishwarath couldn't control himself any more either and, taking Vasishth's permission, put the first morsel of food in his mouth. His eyes popped in amazement. Never before in his life had he tasted such nectarine food!

He had assumed that the prodigious quantities required to feed hundreds of men, that too at such short notice, would mean compromising with the taste but he couldn't have been more incorrect in his assumption. This food could put to shame even the head chefs in his royal kitchen.

The simple long-grain steamed rice gave off the enticing aroma of saffron and cardamom while the lentils had been simmered slowly on a wood fire, cooked in gravy of tomato, nutmeg and cinnamon, imparting to it a heavenly taste. The soft baked bread was perfectly done in a clay oven and was served with dollops of clarified butter while the yoghurt was of such sweet taste that it seemed to have been made out of ambrosia.

To wash it down they were served panna made of mango pulp, and the cheese and stoned peaches offered as dessert seemed to have come from Indra's own gardens. By the time Vishwarath had finished his meal, he was burping with satisfaction.

'My lord,' he said to Vasishth, unable to control his emotions, 'I am sure I speak for all my men when I say that the food we had today was undoubtedly the best we have ever tasted in our lives!'

The Brahmarishi looked indulgently at the king's face where satisfaction and disbelief seemed to be present in equal measure. He accepted the compliment graciously and said, 'It is a matter of great honour for us that our humble ashram was able to provide the king and his men enough food to satisfy their hunger. I know Kshatriyas are generally fond of meat and intoxicants but here we follow strict principles of vegetarianism.

My wife had worried whether we would be able to satisfy your taste buds but we are glad to see that you found the food to your liking.'

Vishwarath shook his head and said, 'O learned sage, the thought that I was missing on meat or wine did not even cross my mind! This food was so delicious that I could happily turn vegetarian just to have it every day!'

Then he asked the sage, 'Please satisfy my curiosity and tell me how so much delectable food was prepared at such a short notice?'

The patriarch answered, 'As I mentioned earlier, Rajan, we have been blessed by Shakra with a gift that provides us the ability to cater to the needs of each living being that comes to our threshold in need.'

Vishwarath asked half-jokingly, 'Brahmarishi, has Indra gifted you the wish-fulfilling Kalpavriksh from his own gardens?'

The sage just smiled, leaving Vishwarath completely flummoxed. Taking pity on him, Vasishth offered to directly introduce him to this gift. He gestured for the king to follow him and asked Shaktri to accompany them.

The three walked towards the stables where Vishwarath saw all his animals being taken care of lovingly. The ashram acolytes were tending to their wounds and massaging their limbs with soft muslin while the notes of soft music flowed from another hut nearby.

As they turned a corner, Vishwarath saw a huge frangipani tree spreading to the heavens, showering the ground with its yellow and white blossoms. He wondered how a tropical tree could grow so luxuriously in this Himalayan terrain but his doubts were pushed aside by the intoxicating fragrance of its flowers that beckoned him. The enclosure below it was fenced and whatever was being protected inside was not visible from this angle.

Vishwarath's heart was racing now; he wanted to see this magical creature that fulfilled the requirements of this ashram and quickened his steps. As he neared the enclosure, the sight of what was inside almost stopped him dead in the tracks.

Inside the fencing, there sat a creature of such magnificent beauty that he could only believe he was dreaming. What amazed him most, however, was the fact that it wasn't an alien plant or animal from Swarg, but a milk-white cow with magnificent golden horns and large flapping wings!

He looked at the Brahmarishi dumbfounded and then at his son. Both sported identical grins on their faces.

The patriarch explained, 'My king, this is the boon of Indra—the divine cow Nandini, the daughter of Kamdhenu, the wish-fulfilling cow obtained from the Churning of the Cosmic Ocean at the end of the last Manvantar.

'Nandini, just like her mother, is a wish-fulfilling angel who can provide whatever the ashram requires and has not failed us yet. In return, the entire ashram cares for her like a mother.'

Vishwarath stood rooted to the spot, trying to make sense of what he had just heard. He was stumped by the existence of a wish-fulfilling creature from heaven, residing in his own kingdom without his knowledge!

Surely, the place of such a magnificent creature, and such a useful one at that, was in the royal palace and not this remote ashram where no one had access to her gifts except a few half-naked ascetics. Something had to be done to change this scenario.

Adhyaye 16

Together they bowed to the divine cow who sat comfortably on a bed of flowers and seemed to have a halo around her head. Her pupils were flecked with gold and her big eyes were adorned with thick golden lashes that seemed to watch every movement of the king.

Her large wings were folded but Vishwarath could see that if she opened them, they would easily carry her weight and take her wherever she wanted to go. He wondered how they communicated their needs to her and asked Shaktri.

The young rishi replied, 'My liege, there is no formal procedure to approach the divine cow; all we do is request her in our minds for whatever is required and it appears before us by her grace. But whatever we ask for must actually be needed and not asked for in greed, only then it shall be provided.'

Vishwarath thought about this and said, 'I am assuming this holy cow figured out that my men and I were famished so when you requested, food appeared in appropriate quantities for everyone. She also judged the needs of our animals hence the medical attention they are getting. This is nothing short of a miracle! I hope you know the significance of this, Brahmarishi?'

Vasishth was not an ordinary mortal and knew the thoughts that were swirling in Vishwarath's mind. He recognized the dangerous path the king was about to tread and said firmly, 'My lord, I know the desire that is germinating in your mind but let me caution you right at the outset: Nandini is not the property of this ashram; she lives here of her own volition. We have no more the right to let her go than one could let go of a person of their own family.'

Shaktri was bewildered by his father's unexpected words and looked to him for clarification.

The Brahmarishi told him what was going on in Vishwarath's head. 'Our king is thinking about the immense use that a magical creature like Nandini could be put to if her ownership were transferred to him. I am simply informing him that this divine cow is not a food-producing machine that we own but a gift from the king of Devas and has a mind of her own.'

Shaktri felt enraged at such a suggestion and said heatedly, 'O king, Nandini goes where she wants to and stays with us out of her own choice. The mere thought that she could be taken away from the ashram is sacrilegious!'

Vishwarath lost his cool too. 'Rishi putra!' he shouted. 'How dare you talk to your king in this manner? I am respecting the Brahmarishi's word since he is my elder and more knowledgeable than me but you should not forget yourself when addressing me. As a king it is my duty to think about the welfare of my people and to keep their needs above the needs of a few hundred ascetics who have anyway distanced themselves from the society!'

Shaktri glared at the king and replied in an equally haughty manner, 'I speak to you in my authority as a man of knowledge to a man of arms. A Brahmin has no obligation towards any Kshatriya unless his actions merit respect and what you are suggesting does not merit any respect from me.'

The king's eyes bulged in disbelief. Never in his life had anyone dared to talk to him in this manner. He reached for his scimitar then realized all weapons had been left outside the ashram boundary.

Vasishth realized the dangerous turn this situation was taking and intervened, 'Shaktri, do not forget that a king is the representative of Indra on Earth and therefore also called Narendra. I understand your anger at the king's suggestion but you must apologize to him this instant for your rudeness.' And turning to Vishwarath he said, 'At the same time, I would like to remind the king that the hermits of this ashram are also your responsibility for we too reside in your kingdom.'

Vishwarath ignored the Brahmarishi's words and concentrated on putting Shaktri back in his place. 'So you think that I do not deserve any respect for thinking about the welfare of my extended kingdom as opposed to a few lucky citizens living here? You think your need is greater than that of the rest of my subjects? What gives you that right?'

Shaktri knew the king was trying to provoke him so he controlled his tone while replying. 'Rajan, my objection to you taking Nandini away is not based on any notion of personal greed. Nandini is a gift to my father and etiquette declares that he cannot give her away without consulting Indra.'

He paused and measured his words before continuing. 'That is the reason according to Dharma but I'll also share the reason that has personally caused me distress. Nandini is not a mere cow but a sentient being with more knowledge than either you or me and no one but she can decide where she lives. Do not forget, her mother is the matriarch of all bovine species and her calf is the vehicle of Lord Shiv Shankar himself!'

Even though Shaktri had presented a morally correct argument, Vishwarath did not want to listen to it. Now that he had set his mind on obtaining Nandini, nothing else would satisfy him.

He further argued, 'If a gift is better used by someone other than the one who received it, why should it be necessary to take anyone's permission? It would be in the interest of the original giver for his present to be utilized well.'

Vishwarath's mind was calculating the expenditure he would save by using Nandini to take care of his army's needs. He would be free of the one limitation any army faces in a foreign land, that of sustenance and replenishment, and would not have to worry about the logistics of mounting even the greatest military conquest.

To counter Shaktri's second point he said, 'As this creature lives in my kingdom, her free will has no significance against the orders of the king. I hereby declare that this divine cow is royal property and order my soldiers to take her away to Kanyakubja.'

As an afterthought, he added, 'In return for the loss to the ashram, I shall provide you with a hundred milk-giving cows from my personal stock and a hundred gold coins every month to take care of your requirements.'

Shaktri was stunned into silence by the king's arrogance but Brahmarishi Vasishth roared like a lion, 'King Vishwarath, have you turned so blind with desire that you can't see reason? You wish to offer material riches to ascetics, hoping to bribe them into doing what you want?'

Vishwarath looked at the change in the old man's features. His face had turned red with anger and his eyes blazed with a fire that he found daunting. However, he could not let these hermits best him in an argument in front of his own men; that would just undermine his own authority.

He whistled to his soldiers to come to him while Vasishth declared, 'O fool, now that you have dared to do the unthinkable, be prepared to deal with the consequences.'

Saying so, he turned towards the cow and prayed, 'Mother, as a Brahmin monk, I have vowed not to take up weapons ever in my life, hence I request you to protect yourself as best as you can. Please do what you deem is right for the protection of this ashram as well as yourself!'

Vishwarath's soldiers were rushing towards the enclosure where the cow now stood in attention. Suddenly, a bolt of lightning struck the ground where they stood, vaporizing them in an instant. Vishwarath watched in disbelief as six of his ablest soldiers were turned into ash right before his eyes!

Adhyaye 17

As he ordered more men to grab the cow, a blinding flash emanated from the cow's mouth and nine soldiers dressed in alien armour appeared, stepping in between Nandini and the king's men.

The divine soldiers stood at least eight feet tall and radiated a distinct glow that identified them as the denizens of Swarg. Their armour had the insignia of Indra on the chest plate—a silver thunderbolt demanding attention on their black outfits.

Each of them carried a shield and spear and wore sturdy helmets that protected their faces, leaving a rectangular slit covered with a visor that they could look through. Standing shoulder to shoulder, the giants blocked the way to Nandini's enclosure like a solid wall.

At first Vishwarath was stunned and realized he may have actually bitten off more than he could chew. He recognized them as the Soldiers of Swarg, the SOS, a troop of highly advanced commandos that Shakra, the current Indra, used to safeguard his interests on Earth.

But then, he thought, his soldiers had just won three major and two minor wars; if they could not face these adversaries here and now, he might as well give up his plan of becoming the universal monarch!

He ordered his men to surround the enclosure and, as they moved to encircle the fence, eighteen more of the battalion appeared with a flash on the other side of the enclosure, forming an impregnable protective circle around Nandini.

A rumble, like that of the thunder clouds, emanated from her throat as she addressed the king for the first time.

'O foolish human,' she said, 'your arguments are tenuous and their logic flawed. What right does a king have on a hermit's wealth that is acquired through intense tapas? It is not someone else's kingdom to conquer and enjoy as the spoils of war. A sage's wealth cannot be taken away for a king's avarice and neither can a celestial being be subject to the laws of this land.'

To the stunned soldiers she said mockingly, 'Try with all your might, little soldiers. I am perfectly capable of defending myself against any use of force.'

It took the men a moment but they gathered their wits and assumed a well-rehearsed attack formation within seconds. They were the best-trained army in the whole of Aryavarta. Vishwarath ordered them to charge at the SOS and attack to destroy the cow that had dared to mock them. At his command, his men advanced towards the towering alien soldiers, their weapons at the ready. No sooner had they reached the protective circle and plunged their swords and spears forward than the aliens' huge shields locked with each other, forming a metal wall that could not be breached.

Vishwarath's soldiers tried with all their might but could neither dent a single shield nor break the hold of any of the defenders. Tired, they had just paused to take a breath when a laser beam shot out of each of the shields and turned the soldier standing in front into a heap of ash!

Vishwarath watched in disbelief as more of his most

capable men vanished in a puff of smoke right in front of his eyes yet again.

He shouted to his soldiers to get back to safety and ordered the archers to shoot above and below the cover of the SOS shields. His tactic gained them some ground as a few of the celestial soldiers fell to poisoned arrows shot at their ankles but then the shields fired again and found every single archer with precision.

Vishwarath told his remaining archers to hide behind the huts and continue shooting while Vasishth and Shaktri watched in horror as their ashram was destroyed in the process. The huts and stables could be rebuilt but they could not lose Nandini to this arrogant human and any steps she took to safeguard herself were more than welcome.

The archers kept shooting and the SOS retaliated by firing sharp, short arrows from their shields. The sharp missiles were heat sensing and found their hidden targets, slicing clean through bone and sinew alike. Soon, another flash emanated from the enclosure and a new platoon of four-armed SOS appeared in front of the earlier one, forming an outer circle of offence.

A hundred chosen soldiers from Vishwarath's army then rushed at the aliens with a myriad variety of weapons to avenge the deaths of their comrades. They were countered by the new platoon that wielded tiny bows that shot numerous rounds of flaming ammunition, instantly incinerating whatever they fell on.

It seemed the celestial soldiers did not like to create a mess, preferring to wipe out every trace of their enemy. Soon, in place of Vishwarath's soldiers stood heaps of ash that were being dissipated by the wind while he stood alone in front of the towering hulks who now pointed their weapons at him.

Brahmarishi Vasishth intervened, addressing Nandini with folded hands, 'Holy mother, you have proven your might and all the soldiers of this king have already joined their maker. I request you to let him go unscathed as the welfare of an entire kingdom rests on his shoulders; let him go for he himself does not realize what his hubris has led him to do.'

The divine cow gave out a bellow of triumph and the defending soldiers laid their weapons down. They would not leave her side till they had ensured the king's departure, hence they surrounded Vishwarath and nudged him to start walking towards his unicorn.

Utterly dejected, Vishwarath mounted his only remaining possession and turned its reins around to head towards his capital. The rest of his animals were left behind in the ashram which now seemed to resemble a zoo more than the peaceful sanctuary it had been.

His face was red with anger and his eyes stung with tears he dared not shed to maintain whatever dignity he had left. He took one last look at the ashram and vowed to return to avenge this defeat. The father–son duo would pay for his humiliation.

Adhyaye 18

Vishwarath rode back to his kingdom, devastated with the turn of events.

He had hoped to enter his capital city to the sound of celebration and revelry, riding on the shoulders of his closest generals, but now he entered stealthily in the darkness of night. He was distressed at the loss of men, especially the hundred who had been his personal bodyguards, and knew he would have to answer to their families for the utterly useless waste of their lives.

But he was in no mood for introspection right now. He would let the anger within him simmer and give him the fillip to attain his goal. He headed straight to the palace of his chief queen and asked to be taken care of. After he had been washed and fed by tender hands, he went to the queen's bedroom to satiate his lust.

As he lay down in his own bed later, he thought of how he could extract revenge from the arrogant rishis. He would have to fight their fire of self-righteousness with a fire of his own, with a force that was capable of withstanding the kind of attack he had witnessed. To do that, he would need access to divine weapons. Only then would it be a fight amongst equals and he would see how Indra's soldiers fared then. He fell asleep planning his next steps and woke up in the morning with a quiet resolve.

Taking a quick bath, he headed to his sister's palace to inform her about the events of the previous day since no one except him had lived to tell the tale. He gave her an almost step-by-step description of what had happened at that unlikely battlefield and Satyavati felt miserable about the soldiers who had been reduced to embers.

Vishwarath asked for Yamdagni so that he could consult with him regarding the next course of action. While they waited for him he also called the sons from his three wives to meet him there. The long years of planning and executing his ambitious campaign meant that he had not seen his three children since the time they were born!

They went to the portico to wait for everyone to come as Vishwarath was meeting them after a long time and he wanted to spend some quality time with his boys before focusing on the problem at hand.

It was a lively veranda, with a peacock perched majestically at one end and parakeets creating a ruckus on the mango trees around it. The area was shaded from the sun by means of cane drapes and had fragrant creepers along the side walls.

As a child he had loved the view from there for he could see the huge gardens as well as look upon the towering spire of the royal court where his father used to sit. Even now there was a veritable riot of colours in front of his eyes and he could see orange gulmohar, yellow amaltas and purple jacaranda in full bloom.

The boys arrived, accompanied by their mothers, and he hugged each one of them, taking time to ask about their welfare. It gave him great pleasure to see the princes growing up so fast and he made all three sit on his lap as their mothers watched indulgently.

Addressing them he said, 'Madhu, Deval and Ashtak, you know you are your father's pride. I am so glad to see you boys after such a long time and I hope you understand the reasons for my absence.'

The boys nodded in unison and the eldest, Deval, said, 'We know that you have been fighting great wars and defeating our enemies, father. We have heard the bards singing tales of your bravery and our mothers keep telling us to become great kings like you.'

Vishwarath smiled and looked at his sister who stood behind his sons. It was her idea to send the bards with him to the battle and have them compose poems glorifying his exploits. After each victory, the bards would return to the city and spread the tales of their king's valour amongst the citizens who would flock to hear the latest news from the battlefield. This way, the citizens did not forget their king and his triumphant battles would also dissuade anyone else from planning a coup.

Satyavati returned the smile and said, 'Yes, my dear brother. Every child in Mahodayapur knows about your exploits and at least half of them want to follow your footsteps.'

He laughed and said, 'I hope the interested half grows up fast as we have many new kingdoms to conquer! This, after all, is just the beginning.'

He looked directly at his sons and said, 'There are many new frontiers to explore and my sights are not limited to the kingdoms of Nabhivarsh. My eyes are on the lands beyond the mighty Himalayas in the north and the island countries in the southern ocean. I want you all to practise your craft diligently and be good, obedient sons to your mothers. Will you do that for me?'

All of them nodded and, after hugging each one again, Vishwarath sent them off with his wives. He then turned to his nephew who had arrived and quietly stood in a corner, and asked him and his sister to accompany him for a walk.

As they took a leisurely stroll amid the potted ferns and dwarf trees that Satyavati liked to cultivate, he shared with both of them what was troubling his mind. 'Sister, I have always looked upon you with great devotion since the time I was a young boy playing with Yama in our garden. I never knew the difference between you and our mother because you always treated me like your own son.'

Satyavati wanted to respond but instead of replying with words just nodded and let her brother do the talking. Vishwarath clearly had a lot on his mind after the recent encounter with the Brahmarishi and she wanted him to share the burden without any interruption.

He looked at Yamdagni and said, 'All through my life, I have never ever encountered any obstacle as insurmountable as the situation I met with at Vasishth's ashram. It's not that our lives have been very smooth and you know that! Living away from our families in the lonely confines of the Himalayas, surviving on the food shared by the locals and berries and tubers collected from around was a far cry from the comforts of palace life.'

Yama nodded and Vishwarath continued, 'Working on my body and mind day in and day out, fulfilling all directives given by our honourable guru and even marrying as per my father's wishes, none of this has come very naturally to me.'

'Yet, I never gave anyone a chance to complain. I married the princesses my father selected for the sake of our kingdom and am not ashamed to admit that I do not really love any of them. I never wanted children, yet I fulfilled all my obligations towards the kingdom by producing not one but three potential heirs.'

Satyavati came to a sudden halt on hearing this. She looked at her brother who was confessing all these things to anyone for the first time and understood how difficult it must be for him to do so.

She made him sit on a nearby bench and said, 'No one's life is a bed of roses, my brother. However, I had no idea that you felt this way about marriage and children!'

Vishwarath nodded and said, 'Believe me, sister, till date, the only desire I have fulfilled of my own was to wage this war and winning it made me feel for the first time that I was fulfilling my destiny.'

He looked at his sister and nephew to see if they comprehended and both nodded in understanding.

'I knew from my childhood that the throne was mine but I wanted to attain that which was out of my reach and the recent victory gave me the feeling of achievement I had been lacking till now. But the moment those Soldiers of Swarg appeared at that confounded ashram, I knew we were licked.'

His face twisted in a grimace and he said, 'How can an average human soldier fight these bloody aliens who have more strength and better technology than us? More importantly, is it even fair for them to stop me from taking something that should rightfully belong to the king?'

Satyavati thought for the appropriate way to respond.

Hesitantly she said, 'Dear brother, let me be very frank with you as regards what happened in the hermitage. When you approached the divine cow with the intention of appropriating her, you were thinking only as a king. You are right in that everything in a kingdom belongs to the king nominally but Dharma does not give a king the power to take away a subject's possessions just because he likes them more.'

Her brother started to say something but she stopped him. 'I know your thoughts were not selfish but for the benefit of the kingdom. Still, a *good* king does not threaten his subjects to obtain something that he desires. Numerous kings have done that in the past for numerous women, a piece of land or something that they valued but they have all paid for it with more than their pride. You were lucky to have escaped unscathed due to the intervention of the Brahmarishi.'

Vishwarath's face burnt with embarrassment at the painful memory. He shook his head to clear it of the images of his favourite soldiers being reduced to ash and shut his eyes tightly.

Taking a deep breath he countered, 'I know I overstepped my boundaries when I treated the divine cow like an animal. But I do not regret for a single moment the steps I took after that. What gives the Devas a right over all such divine creatures? What use do they put them to after all? This Indra has in his possession a wish-fulfilling tree, a wish-fulfilling cow and a flying six-tusked elephant and all of them were obtained by his predecessor's efforts! Has he ever used any of them for the benefit of mankind?'

The blood in his veins was again boiling. 'Devas claim to be the protectors of lower beings, yet they do nothing to help us unless we bow down in supplication to them. Why should we consider them superior to us; they are vain, miserly and show nepotism. All the qualities they claim to disdain in humans are in fact more pronounced in them!'

Satyavati did not like the way this conversation was going and immediately hushed her brother. 'Stop, Vishwa! Do not let your anger get the better of you!'

Vishwarath stopped but kept glaring balefully in the distance. After some time he said, 'I shall stop for the sake of your reverence for them but I have decided to prove that a human can equal these Devas in all respects. I have decided to make my sons the king designates for the three conquered kingdoms while you, my sister, shall become the queen regent of Mahodayapur.'

Satyavati looked at him in disbelief but he seemed more determined than she had ever seen him before. Yamdagni asked a pertinent question, 'How will you prove your worth to them? Go and fight Shakra himself?'

'No,' Vishwarath replied. 'I will not fight anyone again till I have obtained the mastery of divine weapons such as the ones used by Indra's soldiers and for that I have decided to conduct a Vishwa-jeet Yagnya.'

He took his sister's hands in his and said, 'You wait and watch, dear sister. I shall find a way to bring these gods to their knees and accept our equality. Future generations will remember your brother as the man who challenged the gods.'

Satyavati had a deep sense of foreboding but nodded in acquiescence. At least her brother would desist from any more military campaigns for the time being and the kingdom could return to normalcy.

She and Yama still had time to change his mind and it was not necessary that Vishwarath would be able to achieve what he desired. After all, who knew how this proposed yagnya would eventually turn out!

Adhyaye 19

The entire city of Kanyakubja came together to organize the grand yagnya that their king had planned.

Older citizens remembered the time when Kushanabh had performed the notoriously difficult Putra-kaam-eshti sacrifice to obtain Kadhi. Now, Kadhi's own son was attempting something even bigger, a yagnya not to obtain an heir but to gain victory over the world.

He had explained in the open-for-all meeting that he desired to obtain Divya Astras, divine weapons of mass destruction to safeguard the kingdom, and convinced everyone that it was a good idea. The younger lot, who had never seen anything remotely magical in their lives, were excited and volunteered in large numbers to help with the arrangements.

Sages and magi were invited from all over the kingdom as well as the newly annexed territories to be a part of this grand ceremony. It fuelled the positive sentiment in Mahodayapur, and also served to remind the conquered kingdoms that their new ruler was getting stronger and thoughts of a rebellion should not cross their mind.

A huge area was cleared right outside the royal gardens and a massive marquee set up for the ceremony. Sitting arrangements were made for the one hundred and one sages who would be chanting mantras day and night into the central vedi. Acharya Dhanu was made the grand sire of the ceremony and Yamdagni was appointed the chief priest.

Huge stores of sacrificial offerings, camphor, fresh fruit, beetle nut, saffron, kumkum, turmeric powder, sandalwood paste, marigold flowers, mango leaves, coconut fruit, plantain shoots, ghee, milk and Ganga jal had been arranged to ensure there would be no interruptions due to short supply of any of these frequently used products.

Guards were posted outside the arena to ensure no unauthorized person got in to disrupt the ceremony though every citizen of Mahodayapur was allowed a free tour to see the yagnya with his own eyes. Vishwarath had also been observing a fast from the very first day of the ritual to ensure purity of his thoughts and actions.

This morning, he had woken up with a premonition. Somehow he knew that this forty-fifth day would bring culmination to this massive exercise he had undertaken.

He took a cleansing bath, said his prayers and moved to the sacrificial arena excitedly. The rishis responsible for the morning offerings had already taken their place, relieving the ones performing salutations through the night.

He took his usual place and was pleased to see it was the turn of his favourite wife to sit beside him. All Vedic sacrifices for householders required the presence of the man and the woman of the house for fulfilment and Vishwarath's three wives had been alternating every day.

As the first praher of the day passed, there seemed a change in the character of the flames leaping from the altar. The usual yellow-orange flames were turning blue while the temperature inside the marquee was dropping perceptibly. It seemed the yagnya fire was drawing in energy from its surroundings!

Outside, a hush seemed to have fallen on the city and the sun was obscured by dark clouds. The royal garden behind the yagnya precinct that used to be full of chirping birds now seemed to be bereft of any life.

Vishwarath and others present at the altar knew this was a build-up to something stupendous and felt goosebumps rise on their skin. As Yamdagni poured the last oblation for the praher into the holy fire, it seemed to leap out of the altar and jump towards the sky!

The queen gasped and Vishwarath took her hand in his to calm her while his eyes stayed fixed at the leaping flame. Within moments the flame had transformed into a column of pure energy rising from the altar all the way to the high ceiling and beyond. Onlookers outside could see the beam extend right up to the heavens and waited with bated breath for what was to follow.

The energy column seemed to buzz with a blue glow and the air around it felt charged with electricity. As the flame grew stronger and stronger, the entire precinct was enveloped in darkness till the only thing that was visible was the glowing embers in the yagnya vedi and the white flame shooting out of it.

A deep rumble began from the column of fire and suddenly a shape, like that of a giant creature made of fire, emerged inside it. Outside, there was a crack of thunder and a bolt of lightning illuminated the interior of the marquee for a brief moment. Every face was frozen in an expression of awe and the king sat completely alert, waiting for the newly formed shape to command him as to the next course of action.

'Vishwarath,' the fire said, 'the gods are pleased with your offerings and have sent me, Agni, to fulfil your desires.'

Vishwarath looked at Yamdagni for directions and, when his brother nodded, he rose gingerly and bowed with folded hands to the talking column of fire.

The voice boomed again, 'Rise, O son of Manu, and open your arms to receive the gifts of the gods.'

The king did not trust his voice and so did not even attempt to speak. Quietly, he extended his arms as directed and waited for the fire god to bless him with his desired weapons.

Within moments, a long spear appeared in the hands of Agni that seemed to be made of quartz and reflected the light shed by the column. It floated through the air and came to rest in the open palms of the waiting king.

'You have desired for the weapons of the gods and, in their generosity, they have shared them with you as a blessing. Receive first this Vayu Astra that can blow tornadoes of such intensity that they will destroy within seconds what your enemies have built in decades.'

Vishwarath clasped his fingers around the spear, surprised that it did not singe his hands even though it looked as hot as molten lava. But before he could take a good look at it, the spear disappeared and he glanced at his empty hands in alarm.

Agni reassured him and said, 'Do not worry, divine missiles stay with their master in an astral form and can become visible whenever you have need of them. Now stretch your hands and accept this Aishika missile that can melt entire kingdoms into glass.'

Another gleaming weapon, shaped like a thick cylinder with a conical end, passed from Agni's hands to Vishwarath's palms.

'Behold, O king, I now provide you with the Varun Astra that can drown your enemy in torrential rains and the Marut Astra that can turn lush green forests into desert within seconds.

'I also give you the Kalchakra, the weapon of Yamraj that can stop time itself. While your enemies are frozen in that moment you shall be able to move around at will and destroy each of them one by one.'

A spherical weapon and two crescent-shaped arrows presented themselves; Vishwarath accepted them gratefully while the assembled gathering watched in awe.

'Stretch your strong arms and obtain the missiles Kapalam and Kankalam that can lay waste to any population of the super human variety including Yakshas, Asurs, Uragas, Nagas and Garuds. Also receive the Mohana that stupefies; Prasvapana, which induces sleep; and Vilapana, which induces heart-wrenching regret in your enemies.'

Vishwarath felt hot tears stinging his eyes as he accepted the weapons one by one; finally, he felt he would be able to teach that proud Brahmarishi and the aliens a lesson.

'Hold in your hands this Paishach Astra that can suck the blood out of your enemy and the Tamasa that creates darkness even in a blazing noon-sky. Receive from me the Shishir Astra of the moon god that freezes your enemy and Tejprabha, the weapon of Surya that can melt any being into its constituent atoms.'

More missiles and launchers were presented along with divine armour like the one worn by the SOS and a chariot that could run indefinitely without horses. Vishwarath knew he could realize the dream of becoming the universal monarch with these but his goal was to defeat Vasishth and Indra's army.

Finally, Agni brought out the last weapon. 'And now, receive the most dreaded weapon that can, in an instant, cause mushroom-shaped clouds in the air, floods in the oceans and craters in the land, killing everything within yojans of its application site. It can wipe out your enemy cities and poison the land for years so that nothing grows there ever. It can change the very building blocks of life and cause grievous changes in plants, animals and humans alike. This greatly feared weapon, the Brahmashir, is now yours to command.'

Vishwarath could not believe his ears!

He had hoped for the Brahm Astra but the Brahmashir was not a bad substitute either. It was the second most powerful weapon in the universe and could destroy any obstacle that he could ever possibly face.

As the last weapon touched his hands the towering pillar of fire spoke for the last time. 'Remember, O son of Manu, you may use these Divya Astras on a deserving enemy that has the power to fight back or in retaliation to an attack on your kingdom. But if you deign to use these on innocent civilians they shall rebound and destroy your own self. With power comes responsibility and do not ever forget that.'

Vishwarath bowed to the divine command.

In a flash, the energy column disappeared and light returned to the assembled gathering.

Adhyaye 20

Vishwarath was back in the pine woods and this time he had come alone.

He did not need an army today as he had the power of the Divya Astras and he did not worry about them rebounding on him since Vasishth was not an ordinary mortal and possessed immense mystical powers of his own.

He rushed towards Vasishth's ashram, galloping on his unicorn, wearing the sleek black armour Indra's own soldiers had worn, confident in his victory. As he approached the area he started shooting fire-tipped arrows at the huts and saw them catch fire. A cry went up from the ashram and he could see the acolytes running out of their classrooms in excitement and fear. Some were bleeding while others had been hurt by fire and he smiled inwardly, remembering the way his own soldiers were killed that day.

Vasishth and Arundhati rushed out of their hut to see what the pandemonium was and understood that the king had come to exact revenge. The Brahmarishi immediately ordered that the entire ashram be vacated and asked Shaktri to take care of his mother and Nandini while he himself grabbed a horse and rode ahead to meet the king.

Vishwarath saw the huge figure of the hermit rushing towards him but kept launching arrows at the huts in the distance. This was his revenge on this infernal ashram and its denizens.

And it had just begun.

As he came face-to-face with the patriarch he challenged him to save his disciples.

Aloud he said, 'O Brahmarishi, you humiliated the king of your own land and destroyed the very soldiers who protect you from other hostile nations. Today, I shall destroy those whom you protect and take away the one object you are most proud of. Call your divine soldiers and let them face me today for I have come ready with weapons that can destroy those invading aliens in seconds.'

Vasishth saw the SOS armour and divined the events that had given Vishwarath the confidence to challenge him in his own territory.

He did not raise his voice though, and replied calmly, 'It wasn't the ashram residents that destroyed your army so why do you take revenge on these helpless Brahmins? Nandini is our pride and this time I represent her defence all by myself.'

Saying so, Vasishth got down from his horse, took the Brahmadand he used to rest his arm on and, in a swift movement, planted it in front of the king's horse.

The unicorn immediately bucked and backed away from the wooden staff and Vishwarath wondered what could have frightened it so much. He reined it in and calmed it before jumping off its back.

Then he raised his bow and said to Vasishth, 'You represent Nandini so why don't I deal with you instead of that damn creature! Be ready to withstand my onslaught, O wretched Brahmin, for I am fully prepared to raze you and this entire ashram to the ground within the next few minutes. Beware, you haughty Brahmin, for this is what comes of humiliating a Kshatriya!'

Before Vasishth could reply, Vishwarath had already summoned the Mohana Astra and launched it from his bow. His plan was to prevent the rishi from using any of his powers by stupefying him first and then slowly torture him to death using the other deadly weapons he possessed.

As his missile hurtled towards Vasishth, creating a sonic boom, it abruptly disappeared as soon as it reached the level of the Brahmadand!

Vishwarath watched in horror as his first weapon failed to even reach the Brahmarishi. He thought it was a trick the Devas had played on him, that perhaps they had given him fake missiles, and launched ten of his normal arrows in quick succession, targeting his enemy's vital organs, but the same fate befell them as well.

When that didn't work, he resorted to the divine weapons once again, summoning the Paishach Astra that could suck the blood out of the rishi like a vampire. But again, the missile could not pass the threshold set by the Brahmadand.

Vishwarath had neither seen nor imagined anything like this. He went on shooting weapon after weapon but, to his utter despair, every single one of them was annihilated by the invisible shield created by the Brahmadand. It was as if a vortex had opened up in thin air that was swallowing each of his weapons and he did not know what to do about it.

What was the power in this staff? It seemed to be made of regular wood that was twisted around itself in a five-feet long projection. At the top of it was a rounded base that was polished to perfection but other than that he did not see anything special in it. He was sure the power vested in it was actually coming from the Brahmarishi.

Still, he wondered, how a mere staff, used by an old sage,

could stop mighty weapons like the Vayu Astra and the Brahmashir! He felt utterly defeated and his ego hurt more than ever. How could this have happened to him after all the preparation?

He had thought this attack through and had been completely prepared to face any kind of onslaught. He had been ready to deal with the SOS and their laser weapons; he had come prepared with weapons that could wipe out entire platoons of those bloody aliens but he couldn't even get past this man-giant!

All the magical weapons he had obtained from the yagnya had become useless before the power of this sage. He dropped down from his steed, completely stumped.

Once the onslaught from Vishwarath was over Vasishth proudly declared, '*Dhig-balam shastra-balam, Bramha-tejo sarvocch balam,*' reminding the king that the power of arms was useless in front of the power obtained through penance.

When his adversary did not look up, the Brahmarishi heaved a deep sigh and said, 'Rajan, all your weapons are futile in front of my Brahmadand because it possesses the power of the Infinite Brahman while the so-called invincible missiles you used, even though of the latest technology, are still material in nature.

'This material world can never encroach upon the spiritual one and the weapons you obtained from Devas can't even scratch the surface of something that exists beyond the four dimensions of this world. The Devas and their weapons exist in the material creation of Brahma, and no object from any of the material worlds can penetrate the Divine effulgence that we identify as the Supreme Brahman, a part of which exists in the Brahmadand.'

Vishwarath felt as though he was back in school and was being admonished for doing something naughty. Not only had the Brahmarishi defeated him without moving a muscle, he was now lecturing him as if he was an errant boy!

'The Supreme Lord is the Parmatma, the super soul whom weapons cannot cut, fire cannot burn, water cannot wet and wind cannot desiccate. The Brahmadand contains a small portion of His essence and cannot be damaged by anything you throw at it. So understand this basic principle and think twice before setting your eyes on this ashram and Nandini again.'

He concluded with a final warning. 'I hope today's lesson will stay with you for a long time to come.'

Vasishth's words stirred up some forgotten lessons from Vishwarath's time in the gurukul about the true nature of the universe. He had taken those theories with a pinch of salt and never imagined them to be this literal. Now, he was learning it all the hard way.

He shook his head in despair; this lesson would definitely not be forgotten easily.

Menaka

Adhyaye 21

Vishwarath returned to the capital a dejected man. The sky was breaking into orange as he galloped into his city in the early hours of the morning.

His grand scheme to humble that self-proclaimed son of Brahma had failed. He was fortunate that he had gone alone to face his adversary and no one in the kingdom knew how complete his failure was. Their faith in him would be shattered if they knew how badly Vasishth had demolished the so-called superior technology for which he had organized such a huge yagnya.

And on top of it, the kingdoms he had recently conquered might be motivated to rebel and reclaim their sovereignty. No, he had to keep this defeat a secret.

While his city slept peacefully, he quietly entered the palace and went straight to his room, followed by the man he trusted the most in this world. Yamdagni's yogic powers had grown enough for him to keep track of Vishwarath's whereabouts and he knew of the king's return even though he was unaware of the events that had transpired at the ashram.

As Vishwarath was bathed and massaged by his personal attendants, he bared his heart to his nephew. 'I am sorry I did not share my plans with you, Yama, but I wanted to do this as discreetly and quietly as possible. Killing a Brahmarishi, whatever the motivation, wouldn't have gone down well with either the council or my subjects.'

Then he shook his head in disbelief. 'So sure I was of defeating that arrogant sage that I took my victory for granted. Yet, it was I who was humbled and humiliated!'

Yamdagni sympathized with his friend's condition but also knew that his actions had not been honourable. He tried to talk some sense into him and said, 'Vishwa, I agree this has been a huge personal setback for you but don't let this distract you from the things that actually matter in our lives. You have a stable kingdom that is thriving under your leadership, your enemies cower in front of your might, you have three strong sons to take care of you in your old age and your dream of becoming a universal monarch is still possible with the use of the Divya Astras you obtained!'

Vishwarath nodded but said, 'I could still use the Divya Astras on other adversaries and become a Chakravarti, but what would be the challenge in that? I find my existence meaningless if, as a human, I have to keep bowing down to beings who do not even belong to our world.'

Yamdagni shook his head and said in a serious tone, 'This is not the right way to talk about a spiritually advanced being like Vasishth. I can feel your pain, for you are more than a brother to me, but your thoughts are completely overwhelmed by your recent experiences and your judgement is clouded.'

Vishwarath sulked and did not retort.

When he didn't get a reply, Yamdagni continued, 'Brahmarishi Vasishth does not command these spiritual forces as a birthright. He has earned them through his own severe penance. He has toiled for eons and honed his telepathic potential to such an extent that he can directly communicate with Indra and ask for help whenever required.

'And remember, the current Indra, Shakra himself, did not obtain the title because he is the son of Aditi but only after he proved his candidature by killing the dragon Vritra and releasing life-giving waters for our world. So when you say that Devas don't help humans unless they are cajoled and pampered, you are ignoring all the efforts they have made to safeguard us humans.'

Vishwarath knew what Yama was saying was true but he could not reconcile himself to being a second-rate citizen of the world. He asked pointedly, 'If they have done so much already why don't they let us humans achieve some milestones now? Why do they have to poke their long noses in our affairs even today?'

Yama smiled at this and said, 'Don't forget, brother, that you yourself took their help to obtain the divine weapons that you thought could settle your score with the Brahmarishi. If they wanted, the Devas could have refused to share their technology with you, yet they did not do so. I would say that shows their sportsmanship and you should appreciate the gesture.

'As men, we may wish to achieve a lot of milestones and reach great heights but, do not forget, in the grand scheme of things, we are insignificant. Gurudev taught us that this universe is but one out of billions of such universes, each with a Brahma of its own, and even these billions exist but for a single breath of Shri Maha Vishnu! Still we wage wars and hoard our possessions as though they will last us forever . . . as if *we* are going to last forever,' he said philosophically.

Vishwarath felt exasperated and finally asked, 'So you suggest I accept defeat and prostrate myself in front of every Deva or, worse still, their obnoxious representatives, the Brahmins?

I am a Kshatriya and a king. All my subjects should bow to me irrespective of their personal achievements for it is I who provide them this secure environment to thrive in. Why should any being living in my kingdom be exempt from this?'

Yamdagni countered him again, 'As a Kshatriya, it is both your responsibility and your duty to protect the other three castes. That is the very reason the caste division exists in the first place, to ensure a clear distribution of labour in society, so we may know our roles in this world.

'If you were to negate your duties, it would force the Shudras to raise arms or Brahmins to till the land and the Vaishyas to become kings. Remember, brother, nothing is more important for a king than maintaining the fabric of the society, especially not his own personal ambitions. Let go of your ego and look ahead to the other opportunities life is giving you.'

Vishwarath could not take it any more and lashed out, 'Why should I do what I have been told to do? Why can't I chart my own course and create my own destiny? I relinquish the throne and all my responsibilities right this moment! Stop me . . . if you can.'

Saying so, he walked out of the chamber while Yamdagni looked at him aghast. He hoped his friend's outburst would be short-lived and instructed the maids to inform him as soon as the king came back. Lost in thought, he walked towards his mother's chamber and found her kneeling in front of the idol of Lakshmi Narayan, praying for her brother's safety. She did not know that Vishwarath had returned so he updated her on the events of the last praher.

Satyavati knew how crushing such a defeat would have been for her brother. Together she and Yamdagni set out to look for him. They found him walking in the garden beside the pool with fountains and blue water lilies. He had cooled down by then and quietly followed them back to her palace.

Satyavati hugged him tightly and then led him to her favourite swing-cum-bed. The slow swinging motion calmed her mind whenever she was perturbed and she hoped it would do the same for her brother.

Vishwarath lay down on the soft cushions of the swing with one arm hanging over the side and other one on his chest while Satyavati and Yamdagni sat beside him.

He spoke in a calm tone now. 'You and Yama have been right all along, sister. I wanted to appropriate Nandini at any cost and her refusal to come hurt my ego. Indra's soldiers who protected her showed me how inferior I was and I vouched to return as an equal to get her back. But in front of Vasishth's staff, even my divine weapons failed.'

Satyavati began to say something but her brother raised his hand to stop her. 'You don't have to say anything to make me feel better. I'm fine . . . But as a result of my humiliating defeat, I consider myself unworthy of bearing the mantle of kingship any more.'

Satyavati ignored his directions and said, 'Don't be so hard on yourself, Vishwa! You can't abandon your duties just because you were defeated by someone who is not our equal in any measure. The Brahmarishi is almost as old as Creation itself and possesses mystical powers obtained through a lifetime of penance. No human being can outperform his abilities or match him in a duel of the sort you fought.'

Vishwarath listened to her patiently so she continued, 'You are the bravest man in Aryavarta today and you possess weapons that make you invincible. Even if you don't use them on anyone, they will still act as deterrents for anyone who looks at our kingdom with evil intentions. This could be the golden era of our kingdom and we can grow it from strength to strength.

'You and Yama can work together to expand our boundaries and your sons may well be the future rulers of the entire

Nabhivarsh, nay . . . the entire Jambudveep! You could become their guides, watch them get married and sire children who will rule the world and lead lives full of satisfaction and happiness.'

Vishwarath smiled at his sister's words and said, 'You have painted such a beautiful picture in my head that I am almost tempted to break my resolve. But if I do that, I will never be able to live with myself. You don't understand the abject humiliation I faced; I alone can do something to get rid of it.

'I cannot accept inferiority to anyone whether it is a Manas putra of Brahma or even Indra himself. I will show them what a man can achieve once he puts his heart into it. I will show them that a Manav can be as powerful as a Deva and as spiritually advanced as a son of Brahma.'

Satyavati and Yamdagni looked in despair as Vishwarath made his final declaration. 'I will not rest till I become a Brahmarishi myself! My decision is irrevocable.'

Further entreaties proved futile and Satyavati realized that the effect of Ruchik's potion was finally showing itself. Her father and Rishi Dattatreya had tried their best to change his destiny but she knew that no one, least of all Vishwarath, could escape his true nature forever.

It was time to let her brother go on a spiritual journey of self-discovery.

Adhyaye 22

The king's decision to renounce everything and become a sage was greeted by his council with panic.

They had a million questions: Had the king contracted an incurable illness that he was willing to leave everything at the height of his powers? He was hardly twenty-five and had a full life ahead! Had he taken diksha from his erstwhile guru and decided to follow him to the Himalayas? Who would take care of the kingdom now? Was the eldest prince capable enough to handle the responsibility on his own? Who would guide the princes in running the kingdom?

Vishwarath explained his decision to them patiently, presenting his logic in a way they could appreciate.

Addressing them for the last time, he said, 'Dear friends, I know my decision has come as a shock to all of you but I believe the time is right for me to leave Grihasth Ashram and begin Vanprasth. My father had prolonged the second stage of the householder's life because he needed to ensure a strong heir for the kingdom; however, I have no such unfulfilled obligations.

'Our kingdom is bigger and stronger than it has ever been before and my children have astute mentors like you to hone their skills and guide them in the future. My sister has graciously agreed to bear the burden of regency to free me from my responsibility and I cannot thank her enough for this. Instead of accompanying me to the forest, my queens will stay with their sons as their guides and emotional support.'

He looked at Yama and said, 'My brother will continue to be the principal advisor to the king for as long as he deems necessary. I look forward to the time when he will be free of his responsibilities and will join me in the forest. Together, we will relive the days of our youth spent in our guru's ashram. Till then, I require good wishes from all of you to succeed in my endeavour.'

His council members, especially the younger ones he had inducted himself, were sad to see him leave. His rule had ushered in a new era of optimism in the youth and for the first time Mahodayapur was looking outwards at the world.

The elders knew that when the time for self-awakening came, no amount of arguments or logic could dissuade anyone. Their king had realized the transitory nature of material things and, after fulfilling his responsibilities, was moving towards self-actualization. They blessed him and asked him to stay in touch through Yamdagni and come back to the kingdom in case they required his help.

He agreed to their suggestions but for now he needed to get as far away from here as possible. He was impatient to forget the ignominy of his defeat and take the first steps towards becoming an equal to his nemesis.

He bid farewell to his family and left Kanyakubja in the garments of a Yogi, leaving all riches and weapons behind. The royal chariot dropped him till the city limits but he insisted on walking from thereon, saying his last goodbyes to the sights of the city he had loved since childhood.

He hitched rides from passing trader carts plying the east–west highway and reached the eastern bank of the Yamuna where he decided to follow the river on foot for the remainder of his journey.

The winding course brought him to Shatrana, the point of confluence of the Yamuna and the Shatadru with the widest river in Nabhivarsh that sustained huge populations along its banks—the Saraswati.

The blue waters mesmerized him, for this was the first time he had seen the sun set in water, unlike the Ganga near his city where it rose every morning. As far as his eyes could see, the river spread uninhibited.

Gritasmad, an elderly rishi, had called her Naditame, Ambitame, Devitame—the best of rivers, the best of mothers and the best of goddesses—and he could now see why he was so moved by its beauty. This was the widest river in Aryavarta, wider than even the Sindhu to its east, and resembled an ocean in its expanse.

Treading the distance between the Ganga near his home and the Saraswati, it seemed he had travelled to a completely different world. While the kingdoms around the Ganga were ancient and established, the cities around the Saraswati seemed brand new in comparison.

Owing to the frequent tectonic upheavals in this region, the various tributaries of the river frequently changed course, flooding old establishments and drying up the resources in others. Therefore, major cities were built at a considerable distance from the rivers though things settled down a little once the tributaries joined the Saraswati.

The confluence was a holy spot, known as Triveni, and the mingling waters attracted thousands of sages and ascetics. Some even considered the combined waters magical though he laughed at their superstitions. His opinion changed when he saw that the water collected from that spot did not spoil even after months and it reminded him of the Ganga again whose waters had the same property.

The rationalist in him realized that both rivers, originating high in the Himalayas, could have the same bacteriophage activity but this logical explanation was challenged by other seers who asked him why the tributaries, which were also Himalayan rivers, did not possess the same activity.

He grudgingly gave in to their arguments and realized it was easier to let their beliefs wash over his scepticism and go with the flow. He spent many days just sitting on the banks of the river, trying to forget his home and family and lost count of the days spent in the company of these sadhus who had no attachments or possessions in the world.

He had never been too attached to anyone except his sister and nephew but even those bonds couldn't keep him bound forever. He had received regular updates from Yamdagni through messengers regarding the state of affairs during the initial days of his journey after which he had felt confident about their future and stopped the couriers.

He had just one aim in life now and he would not go back until he achieved that. His destiny lay ahead, on the path to becoming a rishi and beating Vasishth on his own pitch.

Wandering along the course of the river, he walked till the confluence with Drishadvati, the third major tributary, and was amused by the different types of ascetics he encountered. Some, called Digambars or Nagas, were naked at all times, completely oblivious to societal norms, while others, called Yogis, lived in cities and preached the way to attain salvation for the benefit of the society. Shaivites used cannabis to attain a trance state akin to their lord while Vaishnavas were frequently seen chanting the name of Hari with a rosary in their hands.

He studied the methods of each, trying to figure what worked for him and, by the time he had reached his destination, he knew what his style of meditation would be. He had decided to begin as a Yogi and initiate his penance by practising control over his breathing.

Following the course of the Saraswati, he walked to the mouth of its delta but found it unsuitable for long periods of stay since the river waters frequently flooded the terrain. He then moved eastwards again, following the coast till he came to the city of Lothal, the biggest city of the region that had a huge dockyard for ships coming in from the western countries.

He set up camp there and started following a regular routine of Pranayam and yogic exercises till he attained mastery of the most difficult of postures. After a few months, he realized that he required a quieter place, and decided to go southwards.

After journeying for a few weeks, he finally found a place to his liking—a dense grove near a stream called Mahi, a little away from the town of Vatpatrak. The ocean was but a short walk from there and he felt sufficiently distant from the locals in the small town to maintain his privacy. He cleared a patch in the middle of the forest and began constructing a small hermitage for himself. It was a basic structure with wooden walls and a thatched roof but it was sufficient for his purpose. His experiences at Rishi Dattatreya's ashram helped him cope with the vagaries of the weather and he became more innovative in using the scant resources available to him.

He used coconut coir to make ropes to bind different elements of his hut and took the help of bigger rocks to create a small enclosure outside his dwelling. Over time, he added a small storage space for berries and tubers that he collected as food, a couple of crooked stones as hooks to hang and dry his clothes on and a rudimentary floor made of pebbles from the riverbed.

Once the basics were in place, he set down to the business of meditation seriously. He knew, compared to the yagnya he had performed for the Divya Astras, this process would be long and arduous but he also realized that this was the only way he would be able to achieve his goal . . .

And defeat Vasishth.

Adhyaye 23

Swarg was buzzing with activity.

The royal court of Indra was a hexagonal hall, supported by pillars of anglesite whose prismatic structure reflected light in numerous rainbows. The floor was made of transparent latticed kamacite interspersed with grey senoite tiles to give it perspective. All the minerals were mined from rare meteorites but then no effort was too great for adorning the court of Indra.

Indra's throne, the fabled Indra-aasan, stood at an elevation at one end of the hexagon and was shaped like a huge dragon. On this sat Shakra, the leader of the gods in this current age and he had just been informed of the intense penance being performed by a human.

Vishwarath was so deeply engrossed in meditation that he no longer felt the need to perform normal bodily functions and was sustaining himself by means of the energy generated through his penance. But meditation of such intense nature could create an imbalance in the electromagnetic spectrum around the sadhak. Once the subtle body chakras and energy channels were activated, the bioenergy created a disturbance that was discernible to anyone who had the acuity to spot it. With each passing day, the intensity of Vishwarath's tapasya was increasing and the reverberations were being felt right up to Swarglok.

Shakra was openly suspicious of Vishwarath's penance and had discussed it with the other Devas. While Agni and Vayu, his closest confidantes, thought it to be a mere whim on the part of the eccentric human, Shakra knew enough about him to be wary of his activities.

The erstwhile king had already gained access to divine weapons through the massive yagnya he had performed and Indra and the other Devas had been forced to share their weapons as per Brahma's rules of rewarding the humans who performed such tasks. What more could he possibly want now? Revenge for the humiliation the SOS had unleashed on his army? Ha! As if a puny human would ever be able to match their technological superiority and physical strength.

Shakra had witnessed the Devastation of Swarg during the reign of the previous Indra, Mantradruma, by the Asur Bali. He had heard horror stories about the near fatal attacks by the blonde twins Hiranyaksh and Hiranyakashipu and knew that they had been saved only through Lord Vishnu's intervention.

Devas throughout the ages had done so much to ensure mankind's progress and saved them from the onslaughts of marauding Asurs—he himself had had to duel with the dragon Vritra to ensure that the parched Earth got back its waters—and still these Earthlings found reasons to complain.

Could this upstart human be actually vying for his throne? After attaining the ability to conquer any kingdom on Earth, was he now aiming for Swarg? No, he would not let a mere man take away the position that rightfully belonged to a Deva!

How he wished he could just smite Vishwarath with his vajra and be done with it but he knew that would not do well for his image and his political rivals might get an opportunity to file for his impeachment. A politician should always play his cards right and, after studying Vishwarath's life, he knew just the right way to achieve his goal.

This was something he needed to plan away from the eyes and ears of the council, for he knew what he had in his mind would never be approved by the Adityas and the Vasus. But then, it was his position that was at stake here and desperate times called for innovative measures. His neural pathways had gone on overdrive and he finally hit upon a plan whose first step was issuing an invitation to Menaka, the most beautiful Apsara in the heavenly realm. Her beauty was beyond description and her voluptuous body, gracefully moving hips, long raven hair and deep blue eyes could mesmerize any virile Deva. No wonder, Shakra thought, his wife Shachi was not too comfortable having her around but he had convinced her, albeit with considerable difficulty, that their relationship was purely platonic.

His reverie was broken by the sound of her anklets and, as she entered, her delicious aroma filled his spacious chamber. For a second he looked unblinkingly at her rose-red lips, then gathered all his self-control and said formally, 'Greetings, Menaka, I am glad you could come at such short notice.'

Menaka gave him a seductive smile and replied, 'How could I not obey your orders, my lord? You know I would leave anything to be with you, yet this is the first time I have received an invitation to come here!'

Shakra felt his cheeks turning red and said hastily, 'Ahh . . . well! The invitation was extended for professional reasons, my dear. I want you to perform a really important task for me.'

Menaka loved seeing the blush on his handsome cheeks. Shakra had a high forehead, big olive-green eyes, dark wavy hair and a perfect nose sitting above bow-shaped lips. He was dressed in white robes that accentuated his well-built body in a way she found extremely seductive.

She came close enough for him to feel her breath on his bare chest and said, 'Menaka is more than willing to do anything you ask of her, my lord.'

Shakra blushed at this overt display of wantonness and was more convinced than ever that his plan would work. He took a step back and said light-heartedly, 'Hold your horses, my dear! The task I ask you to perform is to entice not me but someone who would be more appreciative of your feminine charms.'

Menaka's pretty mouth formed into a pout and she asked, 'Does that mean Devraj himself does not appreciate my charms? Or is it that you find masculine attractions more to your taste now!' she finished with a smirk.

Shakra laughed and replied honestly, 'No Deva worth his salt could resist your charms, dear lady. Yet, my resistance has nothing to do with the potency of your magic or my own sexual inclination but is a result of a promise I made to the other lovely lady in my life. I cannot let any act of momentary pleasure ruin what I have with her and I say this with no offence towards anyone, especially not to you.'

Menaka had never met a Deva who was immune to her allures for most of them succumbed to her advances quite easily. She just had to bat her long lashes or run her finger on a Deva's skin and he would melt like a burning candle. Yet, Shakra had a steely resolve she had not been able to break even after all these years.

She changed her tone and said with a deep sigh, 'Oh, such heartbreak! I wish I could just end my life right here. What use is my body if it cannot be of use to my lord?'

Shakra laughed out loud at this display of petulance and clarified, 'Your magnificent body could prove to be of considerable use to me, if you would but say yes to what I ask of you today.' He could almost see her brain cells furiously working behind that seductive facade.

She got rid of the pout and asked frankly, 'So who is it you consider worthy of my attention, my lord? None before you have managed to resist my charms and I doubt there will be any in future.'

Shakra replied in a serious tone, 'The person I am concerned about is not a Deva nor does he reside in Swarg.'

Menaka was surprised but kept her composure. This was something new and she liked the way this conversation was going. 'Interesting,' she said. 'Does that mean you are talking about an Asur or a Yaksha? I would love to try one of those, they're rumoured to have big . . .'

Shakra cut her sentence midway and replied, 'It is neither a demiurge nor a demon that I talk about. It's a human and a very special one at that.'

The Apsara was stunned and sat down on the couch with a shocked expression.

'You wish to have me sleep with a mere human! Me, the most ravishing Apsara in Devalok, go and cavort with a filthy Manav! Is this some perverted fantasy of yours, my lord?' she asked sarcastically.

Shakra felt anger rise within him. 'Be very careful of the words that come out of your mouth, Menaka. I am not someone you can afford to talk to in this manner.'

Menaka realized she had overstepped her boundaries but said indignantly, 'Perhaps that was a tad too direct but what in the name of the holy trinity do you have in mind! Surely this can't be a result of logical thinking for I have never heard of an Apsara being asked to sleep with a human being before!'

Shakra controlled his temper and replied tactfully, 'There is no force or coercion involved and you are free to refuse. I thought only the best Apsara of my court was suited for this task but if you believe that position does not belong to you or that you're not up to it, you are free to leave. I shall summon Rambha to do what you can't!'

'Like hell you will!' Menaka retorted. 'You know as well as everyone else in Swarg that I am the most beautiful Apsara in all the fourteen lokas and that wench Rambha ranks nowhere near me!'

Shakra laughed inwardly. How easy it was to manipulate females.

In a softer tone, he said, 'I know no other Apsara comes even close to you in beauty, hence had invited you, but you do not seem to understand the significance of my call. You raise your voice against me as if I am one of your love-struck Gandharvas. I am the king of Swarg. I could force you to do my bidding, yet I am asking humbly for your help.'

Menaka seemed to cool down with these words and, after a deep breath, inquired, 'May I ask who this man is and why you want me to fulfil his amorous fantasies? I know it's every man's impossible dream to make love to an Apsara, but I don't see why this particular man should get the opportunity to realize it.'

Shakra sat down beside the gorgeous nymph and played with her hand suggestively. 'Just do what I say now and I would gladly answer all your questions once the task is done.'

He knew he could manipulate her desire for him to make her agree to his plan and, more importantly, keep it a secret. He also knew that Menaka was the only real chance he had to get Vishwarath out of the equation swiftly yet surely.

Adhyaye 24

Vishwarath felt great this morning.

His breathing was completely under his control and, with all the practice he had put into his penance, he could now enter a trance state for hours together. His capacity to dive into the subconscious and explore the hidden recesses of his mind was strengthening and his awareness of all external components was growing by leaps and bounds.

He could now sense the divine consciousness pervading the very ether around him and could feel the life force inside every living being in his vicinity. As he turned his mind outwards, he was able to identify each and every animal within a radius of one yojan and that brought him some surprises. He had earlier observed several black bucks in the vicinity but had never seen the cheetah sitting in a tree not very far from him or the python that lay swollen with its prey! It was astounding. He wasn't afraid of the animals for he knew they rarely attacked unprovoked. It helped that he had made it abundantly clear that he was not a part of their food chain by periodically marking the perimeter of his ashram with a mix of chemicals that reproduced the scent of the urine of a mountain lion.

He turned his attention to the plants around and could individually count each leaf on each branch! He could feel the coolness of the morning dew on unopened buds and sense their return to wakefulness as the sun's rays activated their light receptors. For all practical purposes, he was one with his environment and realized the true significance of the term Vasudhaiva kutumbakam—the world is my family.

Focusing on the micro level he could discern a lady bug crawling on the log near his right leg, three mushrooms struggling to rise up from the earth below it, uncurling blades of grass and unfurling fronds of ferns that slowly but greedily expanded their surface area to absorb as much sunlight as they could.

He wondered if he could expand the area under his consciousness to find out what lay below the earth. For a second he was deafened by the cacophony, for the ground below his feet was teeming with life. But as he concentrated, he could identify small burrows occupied by tiny earthworms and a veritable underground tunnel system that had been created by rodents of various shapes and sizes. He moved on to a bigger burrow and felt the consciousness of a king cobra taking care of its eggs that had tiny pulsating hearts within them!

The experience almost overwhelmed him and he closed his eyes tightly to shut out the sounds and sights of the world taking deep breaths to calm himself. He gradually slowed his respiratory rate, entering into a state of deep samadhi. The self-induced trance took him to a trip out of the confines of this forest and he felt himself soaring higher and higher into the atmosphere until he cleared Earth's orbit and shot past the moon.

His consciousness was taking him towards the brilliant ball of fire that was the reason life existed on his planet. It hung in the sky by the powers of Sankarshan, what his guru used to call 'gravitation'. Dattatreya had told him that this was the potency of Sheshnag, who supported the entire cosmos through his powers.

He crossed the revolving planets of Budh and Shukra and zoomed towards the brilliance that almost blinded him. He plunged into it, deeper and deeper, trying to protect himself from the heat that his conscious mind knew could incinerate him instantly. Yet, no harm came to him. He was immune to the extreme of temperature and lack of oxygen and he realized that only his astral body could attain this feat.

As he entered the very core of that star that was burning up its own fuel, he saw a sight that amazed him as nothing ever had before.

He saw particles made of pure energy colliding, merging, taking on a new form and moving outwards to be dissipated into space to give life to each tiny beating heart on Earth and possibly other planets in the solar system.

He wondered what would happen once this fuel was over. Would the star collapse on itself or would it bloat into something bigger, filled with the entire residue. He remembered how the Vishnu Purana described the end of the world, where the sun was supposed to swell seven times its normal size.

The time for that was perhaps eons away, so he shrugged and plunged into the boiling cauldron of smaller molecules turning into bigger ones. There, his astral body assumed the lotus position and he sat down to meditate, focusing on the energy that drove this seemingly unending process.

Energy . . . Shakti . . . the feminine force balancing the masculine matter of this universe. The continuous exchange between the two, represented metaphorically by the divine union of Shiva and Shakti, was what sustained this universe. And would continue to do so till such time as Shiva decided to dissolve it all and give Srishti Karta Brahma new raw materials to begin the process with all over again.

He meditated on the primeval energy source for all living beings, Goddess Durga, whom Shaivites called Gauri or Kali based on her moods and the Vaishnavas knew as Yogmaya. The consort of Shiva for the former and the expansion of Vishnu for the latter was the guardian of this durg or fortress of material creation.

He meditated on the energy that flowed from the sun to Earth and was transformed by millions of green leaves into food that was fit for animals and humans which was further turned into kinetic energy that was used for creating cities, temples, art, industry, sports, literature—in short, entire civilizations.

The same energy heated up land and water differently, creating currents in the oceans as well as the sky, and helped sustain different species of life. When it entered the planktons, it provided food for bigger fish which in turn supported higher and higher forms of life right up to the giant leviathans living in the dark recesses of ocean, growing larger than any land animal could ever hope to be.

Life on Earth was possible only because this continuous flow of energy was shared in just the right proportion, neither too little, nor too much. Without this Shakti, there was no movement as even a stationary object possessed potential energy that helped it move.

His own consciousness was swirling in the flux inside the core of the sun and he felt his body shrinking, till it was small enough to enter the smallest particle. He felt as if he was watching a dream within a dream where he could see his own miniature self, entering a paramanu, an atom.

He watched wide-eyed as the bright light was replaced by a goddess of a form he had never seen before. She possessed five heads that looked in the ten directions and her ten arms held all the weapons of the holy trinity.

He fell down on his knees upon seeing this glorious form of Goddess Shakti and, with folded hands, verbalized the words that were forming in his subconscious mind:

Oṃ bhūr bhuvaḥ svaḥ
    tát savitúr váreṇyaṃ
        bhárgo devásya dhīmahi
            dhíyo yó naḥ pracodáyāt

O giver of sustenance to the three lokas;
Residing in the sun; hidden by a golden light,
From You all proceed, to You all must return,
That we may see the Truth and fulfil our duty
I meditate upon you, to inspire my activities and stimulate
    my intellect.

As he finished his prayer, he fell prostrate at the feet of the goddess whose five faces wore a smile that a mother reserves for her favourite child. He knelt in front of her and searched in his mind for words that would not come. All that he had felt on seeing her radiance had burst out of his mouth and now his mind was blank like a fresh sheet of papyrus.

The goddess placed her hand on his head and blessed him and it was as if a bright stream of energy moved from her divine hands to his forebrain, stimulating his grey cells and forcing his tongue to form a new word.

'Gayatri,' he said hesitantly and the goddess nodded.

That's who she was, the Mother of the Vedas and the embodiment of the combined female energies of the Creator Brahma, Preserver Vishnu and Annihilator Mahesh. The goddess then spoke for the first time in a voice that seemed like a whisper, yet seemed to come from very far.

'You have uncovered the beej mantra of the universe, the primal verse that can turn energy into matter and matter back into energy. You have made a great discovery and this mantra shall now be available for all mankind to meditate on and realize their goal of self-actualization.'

Vishwarath heard the words as if in a daze. Had the goddess just credited him, a novice, with a discovery of such proportions that it could change the spiritual landscape of mankind? This was unbelievable!

As if in response to his thoughts, the goddess smiled and said, 'Yes, call it serendipity or beginner's luck, but you have unravelled the most powerful set of syllables in all Creation that lay hidden from the dwellers of Mrityulok, since the beginning of Creation. Through sheer luck and intuition, you have managed to achieve what even the sons of Brahma couldn't.'

Vishwarath beamed with pride as the real purport of these words hit him.

He had surpassed the sons of Brahma in his discovery, even Vasishth. Did that make him superior to the Brahmarishi now? Was he too now a Brahmarishi of equal stature to his arch-rival? The prospect was electrifying and he felt goosebumps rise on his skin.

Having read Vishwarath's mind again, the goddess' expression turned sombre and she said, 'Brahmarishi Vasishth is a seer of countless Vedic verses and is responsible for taking them to the world at large. Your discovery is but just a beginning though it certainly deserves the highest recognition and for this achievement, I name you Vishwamitra, the friend of the world.'

He heard the name and rolled the syllables in his mouth, testing them on his tongue.

Throughout his life, he had been called by many names—Vishwarath, the name given by his father; Vishwa, the shorter form his sister and nephew used; Kaushik, his sobriquet for belonging to the lineage of Kush. But he liked the sound of his new name best and bowed to the goddess gratefully.

He felt as if he had achieved everything in life! His one act of exploration had made the Gayatri Mantra available to all mankind and he was proud of his achievement. As his conscious mind began filling up with self-congratulation, his subconscious dragged him out of the sun's core, back to Earth. The journey to defeat Vasishth had begun.

Adhyaye 25

Menaka was sulking; she did not like the task that had been assigned to her.

Still, she figured, this was the first time Shakra had requested her for a personal favour and, if she played her cards right, she might be able to use this to her advantage in the future.

She had liked him even before he became Indra and had it not been for that confounded Shachi, she could have been the one riding the Airavat with him. Anyhow, Devas' and Apsaras' lifetimes were long enough for future opportunities and this could very well prove to be the turning point in their relationship.

She had obtained from him the antecedents and life history of the human he was targeting, though he would not tell her why he wanted her to seduce him.

As far as she knew, Devas had always helped humans progress on the path of spirituality and sending her to disrupt a rishi's penance seemed odd to her. She had no idea what Shakra's real intentions were and, if she were to be honest, she didn't really care.

She had taken up the challenge so she was just going to head to this rishi's ashram, complete her task and return to Swarg as soon as possible. Though she was aware that he had recently attained a new title of Vishwamitra through his penance, given her track record, she doubted she would require more than a couple of days to ensnare him and break his vow of celibacy.

Indra had told her to take the help of Kama and the two now travelled together to Earth, giggling as if plotting a prank. Kama was probably the most handsome male in all fourteen realms and she enjoyed his company though they had never had a conversation before. He had numerous stories to share and she didn't even realize when they arrived near Vishwamitra's ashram.

Kama had played cupid to many couples, both human and divine, and he knew how to set the mood well, so he first began transforming the forest area surrounding the ashram into a blooming garden in all its spring glory. Fragrant lilies replaced thorny brambles and timber trees were supplanted by rose vines and kachnar, showering their yellow and pink flowers in the breeze.

The sun went into hiding behind the soft white clouds stacked like bales of cotton in the sky. Cuckoos sang spring songs while lavender lotus buds opened up in the ponds. Vishwamitra did not notice these changes as he usually started meditating quite early but by evening, the entire area around him had metamorphosed into a garden fit for a king and demanded attention. Waking up from his trance, he felt disoriented for a second, imagining himself back in the royal gardens of Kanyakubja. Was it spring already? Of late, he had hardly been aware of the seasons, so he shrugged and walked to the ocean to offer his evening prayers.

But as he proceeded, he started noticing unmistakable changes around him. The texture of the sand seemed softer to walk on. Gone were the mangroves with their ugly upward projecting roots and, in their place, wispy willows swayed happily. The palm trees near the beach were laden with fruit and the fragrance of jasmine and champa was in the air. A sweet melody played somewhere deep in the forest and he felt lighter and happier than he had felt in a long time.

As he offered his final prayers that evening, he noticed that there was someone further along the shore, not too far from him, doing the same. The shadowy figure turned away from the setting sun, and his breath caught in his throat.

It was the most beautiful woman he had ever set eyes on.

Water rolled off her smooth alabaster skin while the evening light played on her exquisite features. She was tall and voluptuous her long hair was tied in a braid that fell to her hips and her wet sari clung to every curve of her body.

She turned at that moment and their eyes met. It seemed to Vishwamitra as if an arrow had pierced his heart and he felt compelled to greet her with a smile. She acknowledged his greeting with a polite nod and began to move away from the bank.

He was overcome by the sudden urge to not let her out of his sight, and in order to gain more time to admire her ethereal beauty, he moved to intercept her motion.

'Namaskar,' he said tentatively.

She paused in her step and turned a shy glance towards him.

He was emboldened and took a few strides towards her while she stood rooted to the ground; the closer he got, the faster his heart started to beat.

Her sun-lit face seemed to be made of molten gold, with a hint of peaches and rose. It was the most perfectly proportioned face he had ever seen and that was saying a lot since the women of Aryavarta were widely acknowledged to be gorgeous even by residents of other kingdoms.

As he came face-to-face with her, she looked directly at him. Her kohl-lined deep-blue eyes burnt a hole in his heart and he staggered a little under the onslaught of cupid's bows. He could not stall her for long without reason, so he said, 'My apologies for stopping you, my lady, but I have never seen you around here before. I assumed you had lost your way so wished to help.'

Menaka smiled inwardly at the ploy he was using. Vishwamitra was innovative, that much she would give him. Evidently, he was not used to having people around and lived a secluded life. She glanced at him shyly and decided that she liked his looks. Though his hair was matted and his beard was unkempt, his handsome features still stood out and the short angavastra did little to conceal his tall muscular body. His deep baritone voice only added to his appeal. Suddenly, the desire to go back to Swarg took a backseat and she realized it would be fun to toy with this human before returning to the monotonous humdrum of the high-society life of her loka. Telepathically, she conveyed a message to Kama to play along with her and aid her in her ploy.

In a soft whisper, she said, 'Rishivar, I had come to this beach with my family sometime in the morning and happened to fall asleep under the cool shade of a tree. When I woke up, I couldn't find anyone and have been searching for them for almost a praher now. I fear now that they have left without me.'

Vishwamitra was stumped. 'How can your own family not realize they have left you behind!'

She looked at him with eyes filled to the brim and said, 'Perhaps they left me behind deliberately.'

He was shocked. 'That is outrageous! Why would they leave such a delicate wisp of a girl alone in the middle of nowhere?'

Menaka's plan was running like clockwork. She let two tears fall and made an exaggerated gesture of wiping them.

'My birth parents died in a boat mishap and I was raised by my uncle and aunt along with their children,' she said. 'As I grew up, they got many proposals for my marriage but the local astrologer predicted that the family I got married into would be destroyed completely. Moreover, he warned that if I stayed at their house after turning eighteen, all their children would die within a year!'

Vishwamitra was aghast at her story and immediately felt a surge of protectiveness towards her.

The girl continued, 'It's my eighteenth birthday today and we had come to this beach to celebrate as a family but it seems that they had other plans all along. Perhaps they thought leaving me so far away, at the mercy of the elements and wild animals, would rid them of their problem.'

He marvelled at her restraint. Even though she had been left behind by the only family she had known, she was still managing to hold onto her self-control. She was really brave, trying to fight back her tears even though she must be terrified. When he had seen her, she had been well inside the waves and her sari had been completely wet—had she been trying to end her life? God knows what she would have done had he not arrived there in time.

Aloud he said, 'It's a shame that they got scared by the predictions of a soothsayer. Half of these dimwits can't even predict their own tomorrows and they talk about you destroying a family!'

He came closer to the girl and put his hand on her shoulder; it was almost as if a current traversed through his entire body. He realized taking her home would invite trouble for his own self-control but at the moment he had no option but to give her shelter for it was almost night.

Lightning flashed through the darkening sky and moments later was followed by a clap of thunder. Controlling the storm within his heart, he said, 'Dear girl, don't be afraid. You may spend the night in my ashram and in the morning we could try to locate your family or arrange for transport back to your city. Right now let us hurry for it seems a storm is almost upon us.

We can discuss the situation in a relaxed manner while sitting in the safety of my humble abode.'

She nodded meekly and started following him. Vishwamitra thought it best to lead the way and make sure she did not slip on any of the bigger rocks on the shore.

Seconds later a downpour began and he again wondered which season of the year it actually was! Though he signalled to the girl to follow faster, by the time they reached the ashram they were both drenched in the rain.

As soon as they entered the hut, he picked up the arani wood he used for lighting yagnyas and built a small bonfire in one corner of the hut. Since her sari was completely soaked he gave her his spare angavastra to change into while he went out to gather thick leaves that he could lay down as her bed. He himself had slept on dry ground since the day he had left his kingdom, yet he knew he would have to provide something more comfortable for her. Things he had never bothered about suddenly became very important. He had a few tubers stored in his hut but she would need something more filling to eat. He foraged the surrounding forest for whatever he could find and rushed home, not wanting to leave her alone for too long.

When he returned, she was sitting near the fire, wrapped in the piece of cloth he had given her earlier that left her shoulders as well as legs partially bare. Her aquiline nose and the rims of her eyes were tinged with red but her cheeks glowed with a fire from within.

There seemed to be a slight chill in the air and he went to sit near the fire as well. He spread his gatherings to dry them and then offered her the few fresh fruits he could find. She took a berry thankfully and started munching on it politely. As she bit into it, the juice trickled down from her lips and slipped along her long shapely neck to slowly reach the edge of the angavastra.

Vishwamitra's eyes had followed that drop of juice all the way to her bosom and stayed fixed there. The now familiar stab in his chest had returned and he felt an ache develop in his abdomen. As he picked up a fruit to eat himself his hands trembled and he dropped it accidentally.

Menaka quietly picked it and offered to him but as their hands touched he felt another jolt of electricity pass through his entire being.

He had not touched a woman for many years now and suddenly his desires couldn't be controlled any more. He forgot his penance, his dream to best Vasishth, and gave in to her ethereal beauty, grabbing her hand and pulling her close to him.

She embraced his bare upper body as tightly as he clasped hers and, in a heartbeat, his lips crushed her trembling ones. A thunderclap resounded and a gust of wind blew in through the window and extinguished the only source of light in the small hut.

As the embers died, they were consumed by an inner fire that could only be extinguished once he had released all his pent-up passion between her loins.

Adhyaye 26

Vishwamitra woke up with a smile on his face.

He hadn't been so close to anyone in years and had almost forgotten how wonderful the warmth of another body felt. Their love-making had felt different too; it almost felt as if it was the first time he had been with a woman!

He had sired sons on all three of his wives and had spent passionate nights in the embrace of various concubines but last night, for the first time, he had felt complete. It was as if they were two halves of a whole who could attain fulfilment only by coming together.

Yet, come to think of it, he hadn't even asked her name!

He looked at the girl lying next to him, her body completely exposed to his sight, and could not help admiring it once again. She was flawless and even in the morning light he could not find any faults or imperfections in her. Her long dark hair spread around her head like a halo and her lips were slightly parted as she breathed contentedly. Her ivory complexion seemed so pure that it might get spoiled with a single touch. Taking care not to wake her up, he stood up lightly and walked out of the hut.

He took a deep breath, inhaling the crisp morning air, and felt the first rays of the sun warming his bare body. The sky had cleared completely and he decided to walk to the ocean for a quick swim before she woke up. He would need to arrange for her transport quickly so that she could go back to her home.

Menaka opened her eyes as soon as Vishwamitra stepped out of the hut. She herself didn't require to sleep for so long since her internal clock was tuned to Swarg's diurnal rhythm. Yet, she had lain there, enjoying the feel of his body next to hers. She was trained in the art of seduction and love-making and it was no surprise that he had enjoyed the night but she could not remember the last time *she* had felt so complete. Perhaps it was because of the boorish wild passion of a human who had denied himself the pleasures of the flesh for many years. Maybe, she thought, it would be fun to spend more time with him.

She got up and wrapped the tiny garment around her body, requesting Kama to present himself. The handsome god appeared before her and said with a broad smile, 'So mission accomplished, I presume?'

Menaka nodded and replied, 'The poor fellow fell for my story hook, line and sinker and you were bloody brilliant with all the gusts of wind and thunder and lightning!'

Kama smiled. 'Pleasure to be of assistance. And mind you, your histrionics were no less convincing,' he said with a wink.

The Apsara shrugged and declared, 'Well, it was no big deal for me. I was born and brought up for the specific purpose of providing pleasure and I daresay that I enjoy every bit of it myself. However, last night was an experience I have never had before and I would like to make the most of it!'

Kama was surprised; he studied her face for some moments and replied, 'As you wish. I shall return to Swarg and inform Indra that you will be spending some more time here. Do you want me to convey a message to our lord?'

Menaka thought carefully and said, 'Just tell him that I shall return once the threat is completely neutralized. I do not believe in leaving things midway and shall come back only when I am satisfied that I have accomplished the objective I was sent here for.'

Kama gave a slight tilt to his head and disappeared in a flash just as Vishwamitra stepped into her line of sight. As he walked towards her, she could not stop herself from admiring his physical beauty again. The clean lines of his body and the tan he had acquired living in the forest complimented his persona. His gait was majestic and she felt as if the king of the jungle himself was walking towards her while she looked on like a helpless doe.

He saw her standing at the doorstep, looking ravishing even in this rumpled early morning state. A smile inadvertently lit his face and, as he came closer, she rushed to embrace him. He was taken aback for a moment but then he wrapped his arms around her as well.

As they stood together, enveloped in each other's arms, the angavastra slipped from Menaka's body and her soft naked flesh pressed against his hard contours. Desire came over Vishwamitra again and he carried her over the threshold and into the hut. As he lay her down Menaka locked her deep-blue eyes with his, proclaiming her consent for what he was about to do.

They spent the next praher making love, their bodies intertwined so as to resemble a single being. Even when they separated, they did not move away and lay next to each other panting. Vishwamitra did not trust his own heart any more and decided to stay silent.

Menaka took the opportunity to further strengthen her plans and said softly, 'I do not wish to go away. I feel complete here and do not wish to be separated from you for a single moment.'

Vishwamitra's heart skipped a beat and he swallowed deeply before replying, 'What happened between us was just a result of our unfulfilled physical needs. I do not think it would be a good idea to continue it further; you have a full life ahead of you and I am already an ascetic.'

'It may be an infatuation but I want to experience every bit of it. What else do I have to look forward to in life anyway?' Menaka looked straight into his eyes, beseeching with her own. 'If you send me back to the city my relatives will disown me and no one will want to marry me. Left on my own, I will either turn into a nun or, more probably, a whore, now that I have tasted the pleasures of the body . . . *your* body . . . and will pine for it if you send me away.'

Vishwamitra smiled at the last sentence and looked at her with kind eyes. 'Your arguments are as excellent as your love-making and it is hard for me to believe you are the same girl I saw crying at the beach, trembling and shaking.'

Menaka returned his smile and said, 'It's not just my own desire, you will be doing my family and me a favour by letting me stay here. If I stay with you without wedlock, it will nullify the curse on my marital life and ensure the safety of my relatives and I shall repay your kindness by taking care of your ashram and turning your hut into a home worth living in.'

Vishwamitra thought about what she had said and knew it was making sense.

Menaka came closer to him and said in a sombre tone, 'I was contemplating ending my life when you arrived at the beach. I did not want to attract your attention and was hoping you would leave without noticing me. But now I am glad that you stopped for it was your kindness that saved my life.'

He pulled her close to his chest and kissed the top of her head.

'The desire for your continued company is driving me mad as well,' he said, 'but I did not want to be selfish by keeping you away from your life in the city. Though letting you stay would probably be the best thing under the current circumstances. However, you will have to at least tell me your name before I officially agree to your proposal!'

Menaka smiled and hugged him tightly. 'I was called Mena by my family and you may call me the same if you wish. How do I address you, my older lover?' she said with a naughty smile.

Vishwamitra lightly pinched her ear and said, 'You may be younger to me in years but I accept you as an equal partner in my life. You may call me Vishwamitra if you so please or give me any other name that suits your fancy.'

Menaka looked at his honest face and said, 'For me, you have turned out to be a saviour in both literal as well as figurative terms and done what even my own family couldn't. I shall call you Mitra, my friend in the truest sense of the word.'

He caressed her hair and then lifted her chin to look at her. She seemed happy and he was glad she was staying. Even though he had left the world and come here to achieve an almost impossible goal, it felt good to have someone to talk to once in a while. He was sure she would get bored of his company in a month or two since he spent the entire day meditating, and maybe she herself would suggest leaving. Till then, he could relive some parts of his old life and simultaneously work towards his goal.

It may turn out to be a win-win situation for both.

Adhyaye 27

Menaka was happy.

Not because she had accomplished the first mission Indra had given her but because for the first time in life she was with someone who truly cared for her.

Her life in Swarg had been extremely comfortable, always surrounded by attendants and admirers. Yet, the feeling of belonging to someone special was completely different. With a sigh she acknowledged to herself that she, the great seductress from Swarg, had fallen hopelessly in love with a human.

Her affection was not because of his physical attributes alone. He was caring and loving and showered as much attention on her as his daily routine allowed, which, she had noticed, he was trying to modify as well. Instead of his usual dawn-to-dusk sessions, he was taking short breaks in between to spend time with her and have their meals together—meals that she had been cooking with his help! Her culinary skills were nothing to boast about since she had hardly ever lifted a finger in Swarg but here she felt happy trying new recipes with whatever limited ingredients they had access to and waited for his compliments. In the afternoon, they would sit under the shade of a large magnolia tree and have their simple meal and in the evening they would sit beside the fire and talk endlessly.

His mystical powers had grown to a considerable extent and he could conjure up whatever material stuff she felt the need for. She now had fifteen outfits to choose from, a stack of utensils for cooking, paints and canvases for passing her time, a veena to indulge her musical inclinations and, most importantly, a mirror that she used to groom not only herself but Vishwamitra as well.

After eight years of sporting facial hair, Vishwamitra was clean-shaven again. She would run her hand over his smooth, chiselled jaw and tease him that he looked much younger than his thirty years.

Together they had expanded the small hut and it was now spacious enough to hold guests even though he often joked that no one would come to visit them in the jungle. She, however, knew that the arrival of a small guest was imminent for they had been having intercourse without any protection since the very first day they had met. The only reason she had not conceived till now was because she had control over her body functions and did not menstruate like the women of Earth. Somewhere deep inside, she had a guilt nagging and tugging at her for even though this man had given himself completely to her, she hid her true identity from him even today.

What would happen if she told him the truth? Would he still accept her or would he turn completely against her in rage?

She thought of broaching the subject indirectly at lunch time and started telling him the story of his ancestor Pururavas who had fallen in love with an Apsara, Urvashi. She had known Urvashi personally and had been one of her few friends before her dalliance with the mortal king. That relationship had ended quite positively for them, for seeing their love Indra had invited Pururavas to stay with Urvashi forever.

After narrating their story she asked, 'Do you think they could have lived happily ever after? Can two people from such diverse backgrounds find happiness to last a lifetime?'

Vishwarath had been enjoying the bajra roti she had prepared with lentils and took a while to respond.

He said thoughtfully, 'If two people are compatible with each other in the broader aspects of life, I don't think their backgrounds matter too much for it is only the less important things that differ in everyone's upbringing. I have personally seen my grandfather Kushanabh and grandmother Ghritachi have a similar relationship. I believe where there's love, people change and adjust according to each other.

'I have lost count of the many moons that have passed since the day I first set eyes on you and, look at us, we are still going strong. Before I met you, the only desire I had was to become more powerful than Vasishth, but now I am content with meditating for my mental peace and spending the rest of my time with you. You have given my life a new pursuit—the pursuit of happiness.'

Menaka's eyes filled with tears. She had been lying to this man for years now while he had accepted her completely into his life and even modified his goals to include her in them. She hoped she would not have to leave him and go back to Swarg, for Indra had been sending missives asking about her return quite frequently. She had managed to stall him by saying the task was still unfinished but he was bound to get suspicious with this domesticated avatar of hers!

Maybe she should make a quick visit to Swarg while the rishi meditated this evening, she thought and, when he left for his evening session, Menaka used her magical powers to access the portal that could transport her right to Swarg. As soon as she arrived, she changed into her usual attire and went to meet Indra.

Shakra was pleasantly surprised and welcomed her with open arms. 'You are here at last! It's so good to see you back, Menaka,' he said with a smile.

She acknowledged his welcome with a slight curtsey and then clarified, 'Yes, I am back, Devraj, but only to give you an update. I will be returning to Earth shortly for my mission is still not complete.'

Shakra looked at her with a frown and said, 'You've been on Earth for many years now, Menaka! What's going on between you and that human? I admit you have done a lot to assuage my worries and kept him remarkably occupied but you have the right to come back and resume your life. Your obligation towards me was fulfilled long ago.'

Menaka smiled; she would have given anything to hear these words from Shakra earlier but now all she wanted was to rush back to her lover's arms.

She replied, 'Yes, my obligations towards you were fulfilled, Devraj, but your mission opened my eyes to a different aspect of life. Coming here after half a decade, nothing seems to have changed and I realize how boring and utterly monotonous my life would have been here.

'Instead, I have spent these years living my life to the full along with that human. I have seen the changing seasons and grown with the years. If you permit, I would like to spend some more time on Earth and figure out the direction I would like to take in the future.'

Shakra was alarmed at this change in Menaka but said equably, 'If that is how you feel, I will not stop you. But do not forget, that the human will die sooner or later and you will have no choice but to return to Swarg.'

Menaka nodded slowly. In the excitement of living with Vishwamitra, she had almost forgotten the short lives mortals had and Shakra's parting words had made her face the reality.

However, she realized she would still prefer to spend more time with the man she loved right now rather than worry about how long he was going to live in the future.

Bowing to Shakra once, she took his leave and left for Earth.

Adhyaye 28

Shakra looked at Menaka's receding form thoughtfully.

He had earlier lost Urvashi, the prize of Swarglok, to another Chandravanshi. He had given in to their love and accepted one human into his realm but he could not afford to lose another one of his Apsaras to this man who in all probability would become his sworn enemy once Menaka left him.

He analysed the situation and decided to call Agni, Kama and Vayu for counsel in his personal chamber. He would need their opinions before deciding how to end this affair without hurting Menaka.

Kama arrived in an instant. He seemed to have risen from an orgy for his upper body was covered with red marks. Shakra smiled; this guy was incorrigible.

Vayu came next. He was in good spirits for he and Varun had been engaged in blowing tornadoes in the ocean and apparently had had a great time. His stocky body was shaking with mirth and his chubby face was creased with laughter as he told Shakra of their exploits.

Agni was the last to appear. He had been a part of a five-year long yagnya being conducted by the Suryavanshi king Mandhata and had returned sluggish and tired, complaining about the copious amounts of ghee he had been fed, turning him round in shape. Shakra laughed at that and asked the three to take seats.

Then he narrated the entire episode from the beginning.

Agni was the first one to react. 'I knew the day I gave him the Divya Astras that he would use them to turn against us but was helpless in the face of Brahma dev's directive!'

Shakra nodded his head in understanding for all of them were bound by the rules set by the Creator in the beginning of Time. Devas were supposed to help any deserving human and aid in their advancement, both spiritual as well as technological.

Vayu had a grievance with the Chandravanshis since the time Kadhi's sisters had refused his hand in marriage. He had no reason to like Kadhi's son now and he agreed with their assessment.

Kama was the only neutral party and he gave his frank opinion. 'I believe we are being too hasty in our judgement of this man. He is ambitious, I agree, but till date he hasn't done anything directly against Swarg. Granted, his attack on the Brahmarishi was foolish but I don't believe he has set eyes on the Indra-aasan.'

Shakra smiled and said, 'You, my boy, have a heart filled only with love. I knew you would play devil's advocate and I am happy to have a difference in perspective to balance our discussion. But do keep in mind that even though Menaka's presence has slowed down Vishwamitra's penance, he has still managed to attain the eight primary siddhis.

'The powers of Aṇimā, reducing one's size to that of an atom; Mahima, expanding to the size of a mountain; Garima, becoming infinitely heavy; Laghima, becoming weightless; Prāpti, access to all places at all times; Prākāmya, fulfilling all material desires; Ishaṭva, absolute lordship above the material world; and Vashatva, the power to subjugate any living being, have made him a siddha and I doubt he will hesitate to use them against us.'

Agni agreed. 'I do believe that these spiritual siddhis will be a useful addition to the physical weapons he already possesses thanks to our generosity. We need to find out a way to break his progress completely.'

Shakra was glad to get some support for his argument and said, 'Your observation is correct, my friend, and that's where my next question is headed. I want to know, Kama, your reading of the bond that exists between the human and Menaka.'

Kama thought for a moment and replied, 'Well, there I believe you may have a problem.'

'What do you mean?' Shakra asked.

'I have taken many missives from you to her over all these years and her responses have always been vague. I had believed her the first time when she said that she would like to stay in order to complete the task to perfection, yet lately I have been getting the feeling that she has fallen in love with Vishwamitra.'

Shakra nodded in agreement and said, 'That is exactly my reading as well. She might have enjoyed the change in scenery in the beginning but now she stays on for her love for this man. I worry that we may soon lose another Apsara to a human and that too our very best one. If this continues, Swarg will be bereft of all its Apsaras very soon!'

All four of them sat pondering how to deal with the situation and, after some brainstorming, Vayu said, 'Why can't Kama remove the effect of his arrows from both their hearts? He fuelled their love, he should be able to take it back as well!'

Kama shook his head and said, 'It is not as easy as you think, Vayu dev. My arrows just serve to ignite a spark but the fire can only flare up if there exists some amount of attraction to begin with. With time, the effect only intensifies and it will be almost impossible to remove it completely after they've been together for so many years.'

Shakra agreed with the logic but asked for a way out. 'If not this, then what else can we do to break this infatuation? For I have a feeling that what Menaka's love could not put an end to, her betrayal definitely will!'

Kama thought about it for a while and said slowly, 'I hate to admit this but I think I have a way to break their relationship.'

All three Devas looked at him expectantly and he said, 'Instead of trying to remove the effect of my arrows, how about enhancing it further? I could stir up the emotion in Menaka's heart to the extent that she feels compelled to come clean with the hermit about her original intentions.'

Shakra marvelled at the ingenuity of Kama's suggestion and gave him a pat on his back. 'Bravo, my friend! I believe you have hit the nail on the head, for this way we are saved the trouble of getting into both Menaka's and the human's bad books while still managing to break their relationship. I am sure the heartbreak will kill him, or at least his spirit, and the threat to Swarg will be neutralized forever.'

Kama received Agni and Vayu's congratulations with a smile, though his own conscience pricked at his heart. He was fond of Menaka and he could not break her heart suddenly. He thought of buying some time for her and said to the other Devas, 'Even though my purpose in life is to spread love, yet for the first time, I shall be responsible for breaking it for the sake of my loyalty towards Swarg. I shall do this only for you, Devraj, but I shall do it slowly and gradually so that it doesn't seem contrived.'

Shakra nodded in agreement to Kama's plan and concluded, 'So be it!'

Adhyaye 29

After coming back from Swarg, Menaka had decided to plunge head first into the relationship to extend its life as much as she could.

For the next couple of years, she devoted herself completely to her paramour and he reciprocated with equal fervour. They had become inseparable and their passion and longing had only deepened. They spent more and more time with each other, making crazy love irrespective of the time and location.

Many a time Menaka thought of coming clean to Vishwamitra but was too scared of his reaction. She was determined to try and prolong the life of this relationship as much as she could, even if it meant hiding her true identity. She could not afford to lose him for he meant too much to her. In order to consolidate their relationship, after years of being together, she decided it was time to conceive a child.

When she gave him the good news, Vishwamitra was ecstatic. He had never been happier in his life, not even at the time of his eldest son's birth for it had meant nothing more than begetting an heir for his kingdom.

He admitted as much to Menaka and said, 'This will be the first child born of my loins that I will truly consider my own!

I am so happy, Mena, that I don't even know how to express myself. You have filled my life with love and supplanted the hatred from my heart completely, and I can't thank you enough for this transformation.'

Menaka didn't have the heart to say anything so she just nodded quietly as tears spilled out of her eyes.

Vishwamitra hugged her and said, 'Do not cry, my dear; we have defeated fate and fate readers alike.'

He reminded her of the time they had met at the beach and how helpless she had been then. 'In spite of what your astrologer had said, we have been happier than most married couples can ever hope to be. And now, I am going to spoil our little daughter and shower her with all the happiness in the world.'

Menaka looked confused with the last sentence and he said, smiling, 'I used my yogic powers to divine the sex of our child. Goddess Lakshmi herself is arriving in our humble ashram.'

Menaka was overjoyed and clung to him joyfully. 'Oh, Mitra,' she said, 'I never imagined becoming a mother could bring so much joy!'

Vishwamitra nodded. 'Indeed, becoming a parent is one of the greatest joys in the world. I am thinking of moving back to the kingdom for your proper care. If you agree, we should make the trip soon, before it becomes harmful for our unborn child.'

Menaka couldn't stay silent any more. Overcome with guilt, she blurted out, 'Mitra, ever since we met, more than a decade ago, I have lived every single day of my life seeing you, breathing you and loving you. But there's a part of myself I have kept hidden from you that I want to share.'

Vishwarath thought she was trying to be funny. 'Yes, I know,' he said, laughing. 'I have never been able to find out the secret of your agelessness! While I have been turning older and older, your skin glows with the same radiance as the day we met and your beauty is undiminished. Come now, spill the beans and share the secret so that your lover can look as young as you,' he said with a wink.

Menaka tried to smile then bit her lip; this was not going to be easy.

She continued the thread he had started and said, 'Have you never wondered why that was so, Mitra? Why my appearance remains unchanged or why I have not conceived for so many years?'

Vishwamitra looked at her quizzically, wondering what she was trying to convey.

'Well, as for your beauty, you are not even thirty and I don't see any reason why you should show any signs of ageing yet. You eat healthy, get enough exercise and have a loving partner who takes care of your every need—in short, your life is stress-free and that is the reason of your glowing skin!' he finished light-heartedly.

Menaka smiled at his logic; men could be so dense sometimes!

She went close to him and ruffled his hair. 'And what about the fact that I had not conceived during a decade of us going at it like rabbits?'

Vishwamitra guffawed at her analogy and said, 'Well, I never had any complaints on that aspect. It is easier for me to live the way I want if I don't have any additional responsibilities and I actually thought it a blessing that you were not conceiving even with our, what you so eloquently call, "going at it like rabbits".'

Menaka felt guiltier than she had ever felt before.

How much this man had trusted her and how badly she would break his heart if she confessed the real purpose of her coming to Earth! Still, she decided, she had fooled him long enough and could not carry on with this charade any more.

She took his hand in hers and said, 'Mitra, you know I love you more than my life and that is why I am willing to risk your anger and resentment by telling you what I am about to say now.' She looked at him helplessly and said, 'I wish things had not started the way they did but I can't change the past however hard I try. All I know is that I cannot lie to you any more. I want our present and future to be different.'

Vishwamitra was genuinely puzzled. 'Different?' he asked.

Menaka nodded slowly and said, 'Not different in the way we love each other for I have never felt so much love in my long life. But different in terms of my honesty towards you.'

'Have you been cheating on me, my love?' he asked with a surprised expression for he did not see how that could have been possible. They lived in the jungle, secluded from the world, and she had spent every waking minute of her life at the ashram looking after his needs. In turn he had done the same, and he had never felt a disconnect between the two of them.

Menaka didn't know how to convey to him the turmoil in her mind. This was the most difficult thing she had done in her life but she knew it had to be done, and done right now for she would not find the courage to do it ever again.

'I am not a helpless human girl who was left behind by her relatives based on some astrologer's recommendation; I am Menaka, the chief Apsara from Indra's court, who was sent here with the sole purpose of disrupting your advancing penance for he felt threatened by your growing yogic powers,' she said in a rush.

Vishwarath looked at her with shock on his face. What was she talking about? He had found her in a pitiable state when she was trying to end her life . . .

'No!' he cried out. 'This cannot be true! Why are you saying all this? Why do you want to ruin this perfect moment?' He looked at her with pleading eyes. 'I have felt nothing but love from you since the moment we have been together. Had you been playing with me on someone's instructions I would have sensed it sooner or later. Do you wish to leave me now? Is this a strategy to do that?'

Menaka was sobbing hard. 'You did not sense my guile, my love, because I was and still am genuinely in love with you. My feelings for you are as pure as the waters of the Saraswati but it pains my heart to admit that I was sent here with a nefarious design to ruin your tapasya.'

Vishwarath's head was reeling; the woman he had accepted as his soulmate was a charlatan! He had never imagined the Devas could play such a cruel joke on him. All this love and affection had been Indra's ploy to make him forget his chosen path. He felt like a fool falling for it the way he did! All the negative emotions he had let go off years ago came rushing back.

His eyes burnt with rage and he rose, addressing Menaka, 'So you played with me all these years? You whore of the heavens! You used my love for you to twist my mind and keep me tied to your bosom! I loved you the way I haven't loved anyone in my whole life and this is how you repay me?'

Menaka was petrified as she saw the change that came over him. She had never seen him this angry and realized her betrayal and the hurt it had caused went deeper than she had imagined it would.

She fell at his feet, shedding copious tears and begging for forgiveness.

'Mitra, please,' she said between sobs, 'I have come clean and told you the truth, please don't break my heart with such harsh words!'

He looked at her contemptuously and said, 'You haven't come clean; you have opened my eyes to how cruel and deceitful you've been! You can cry and beg and cling to my body but I damn you now. You have broken your heart yourself while breaking mine. I can't even convey the loathing I feel for you right now.'

Vishwamitra stood rooted to the ground, fuming at his own stupidity and hating the Devas even more than before. They had humiliated him through Vasishth earlier and now they had broken his spirit using a celestial wench. He had fallen so madly in love with her that he had never sought to find out her antecedents or check her story. They had had such a beautiful life together . . . he had felt complete in every meaning of the word and now she was telling him that all that was a lie!

Blood boiled in his veins and he shoved her away. 'Get away from me!' he roared. 'Get as far away from me as you can for I do not want to hurt you in my rage. Take my warning and run away to your master, you filthy animal. You did his bidding like a slave and in turn made me your slave but I will not be bound by your fake affections any longer.'

Menaka couldn't believe the words she was hearing. This was supposed to be the happiest day of their lives and here she was, witnessing all her hopes and dreams come tumbling down, being treated worse than an animal! She knew she had to get out of his sight right now for the sake of her daughter, else in his rage he might just attack them both.

Vishwamitra sensed her fear and said, 'The only thing you Apsaras are good at is screwing and you screwed me quite well, both figuratively and literally. I do not wish to harm you nor the unborn child so I implore you to leave my ashram right this instant.'

Menaka summoned her inner strength and tried to get up. She had never imagined someone could be this hurt, least of all she, the darling of Swarg.

How had things turned so bad? She knew she had lured him into her trap but she had also spent a long time loving him and caring for him. She had to try to make him understand. She folded her hands and said, 'Mitra, I had no reason to tell you all this even today but I did it out of the loyalty I have for you.

I could have kept quiet and spent a lifetime living this dream and you wouldn't have been any wiser, yet I did it for you, for us, for our love. I have been a whore most of my life but you are the first person I have loved truly, deeply, in a life that is much longer than your own.'

Vishwamitra looked at her with bloodshot eyes but didn't answer back.

Emboldened, she pushed on, 'I confessed today to get rid of the guilt that has gnawed at my heart every single day I have spent with you. I have thought about confessing to you so many times but the idea of losing you was too much to bear and I could not do it. But today is a new beginning and I wanted to tell you everything even if you hate me for the rest of our lives.'

Vishwamitra's anger evaporated but his heart broke down.

His eyes started watering and he looked at Menaka with tears stinging his eyes, 'There shall be no new beginning for us. The only thing I see in your eyes is the laughter of Indra and his coterie of demigods who have watched me making a fool of myself while I thought I was living the perfect life. If you ever really loved me, Mena, Menaka, whoever you are . . . don't show me your face ever again.'

He took a deep breath and said, 'And when you reach Swarg, tell Indra your actions have only served to revive my determination . . . and this time, it's war.'

Adhyaye 30

Vishwamitra had not come out of his stupor for more than a day now.

He was furious at Menaka for betraying his trust and livid with himself for letting his craving for love overpower his mental faculties. Having stayed alone for so many years, he had started to yearn for someone's company and her arrival had fulfilled an unmet need, making him believe he had found his soulmate.

Her confession had shattered his heart into a million pieces and he felt foolish and used. And now, he would have to begin the difficult task of mending. He could not stay at this place even a moment longer for everything around reminded him of her.

The floor was still decorated with rangolis made by her delicate hands and he could almost imagine her sitting there, a vision in off-white, drawing patterns on the floor and filling them with different colours. The cooking pot still contained the kheer she had prepared and he realized she must have meant to give it to him after sharing the news about the baby.

Oh, how he missed her right now! That she had wronged him was undeniable but was his reaction justified? He had kicked her out of their house on the day she had told him she was carrying his child. He felt remorse tear at him and stood up to go and look for her but then reality hit him.

She had just been a pawn in the hands of Indra, and even if he took her back, his heart would never be able to trust her the way it did earlier.

How many mornings had he watched her face glow as the golden rays of sunlight teased her eyelids open? Her shapely arms would stretch towards him but he would deliberately stay out of their reach, tempting her, tormenting her when he himself wanted nothing more than to fall into her embrace.

So many winters they had spent cuddled together in the bed, making love again and again under the pretext of giving each other warmth. Summers had been spent frolicking in the waters of the small river by his ashram, watching flamingoes turn the estuary pink when they visited from the northern countries.

How could he forget her pearly giggles when she was happy and the way her red-rimmed eyes looked at him when he unknowingly upset her! He longed now for their arguments and invariable reconciliations, their longing and loving, their verbal play and physical intimacy. While she played the veena, he would give her company using makeshift drums and they had spent many a rainy evening practising inside.

And now, his life seemed deathly silent, bereft of all music.

He suddenly felt the need to check on her condition and focused his energies on locating her. Soon images started to swirl in his mind and he caught flashes of what had happened to her since he had thrown her out, starting from her limping out from the ashram in a semi-dazed condition.

He saw her taking refuge in the nearby grove where she was received by some forest spirits, followed by a vision of her belly swelling and then a flash of brightness when she delivered the baby. He was surprised; how could she deliver so soon! But then he remembered that Menaka was not human and concluded that perhaps her body followed a different gestation cycle. He tried to focus on the baby, her daughter . . . his daughter . . . the most angelic child he had seen in his life!

He wished he could touch her face, hold her in his arms but by that time he had already moved to the next vision which was disturbing. He saw Menaka leaving the baby at the ashram of Rishi Kanav who lived further inland. Vishwamitra's anger resurfaced and he cursed her for coming into his life. Why couldn't she take the baby with her? With a start he realized that perhaps the baby would cause her to lose her market value! How completely heartless these aliens were; if he had his way he would never ever let a single one of them step on Earth ever!

He felt sorry for the child, abandoned by her own mother and father, and felt remorse for not being there for her. He was relieved by the next vision which showed the baby being taken in by the kind sage and his wife who were alerted to her presence by the shakunt birds of the ashram. With all the yogic energy he had amassed within himself, he blessed his daughter with a future that she truly deserved. She would have a good upbringing, a wonderful life partner and an illustrious son who would unite all the kingdoms of Nabhivarsh and change its destiny forever by giving it a new name. What his own sons may not be able to accomplish, his daughter's son would achieve in the future.

His conscience somewhat assuaged, he shut out his feelings and started concentrating on the task at hand. Perhaps it was time to return home, to the arms of his family. He had not met anyone from his past after Menaka had come into his life but he felt the urge to be with them now.

He had taken well over three years to get to the western edge of Aryavarta but thanks to his yogic powers, he could travel to any place on Earth now with the speed of thought.

He had never needed to use the siddhis before but now he would utilize them to hasten the achievement of his goal.

He turned to take a last look at the ashram that had been his home for more than a decade and sighed deeply.

It was time for Vishwarath to disappear completely and Vishwamitra to take centre stage.

Vishwamitra

Adhyaye 31

Vishwamitra's decision to move to the Himalayas was vetoed by the two people he loved the most so he set up base on the banks of River Kaushiki at a secluded spot not too far from the city of Ayodhya. The fertile Gangetic plain with its dense forests, fragrant mango orchards and lush sugar cane fields was perfect for his purpose. The decision to camp here was a conscious one, for Yamdagni had informed him that Vasishth had been appointed the chief priest of the kingdom of Kosal—of which Ayodhya was the capital—by the Suryavanshi king Satyavrat.

Vishwamitra's proximity to his nemesis strengthened his determination. He did not waste too much time setting up an elaborate ashram and straightaway got to work. Even when with Menaka, he had not completely abandoned his yogic pursuits, hence it wasn't too difficult for him to fall into a routine again.

As he had done a decade ago at the banks of River Mahi, he began the process by controlling his breathing and the practice of complicated yogic asanas. This was followed by gradual progression into advanced stages of meditation and complete non-distraction. His sensory acuity and cognitive function improved and he moved towards development of full mental potential. Days turned to months and months to years but he did not move a muscle and one by one he gave up eating, drinking and sleeping. He was so engrossed in the inner world that his consciousness did not register what was happening outside. His ashram was overrun by creepers and, slowly but steadily, the forest reclaimed what had been taken from it. The banyan tree under which he sat meditating spread its canopy for a mile around, its aerial prop roots giving rise to new trees, gradually converting the entire area into a pillared shelter that protected him from the elements.

Vishwamitra had been stationary for so long that the forest animals now considered him a part of the landscape. His hair grew long and matted and once again a dense beard clouded his handsome face. Without any external nutrition or physical exercise, his muscular frame gradually started losing mass. His cheeks became hollow and the wide torso shrunk so that a passer-by could have easily counted his ribs. Not that he was visible to any chance visitor, for his gaunt frame was by now completely camouflaged by his surroundings. Ants had built an architectural wonder around him and gradually his entire body was covered in mud and clay.

Oblivious to the creatures surrounding him, Vishwamitra dived into the subconscious recesses of his mind and absorbed new siddhis from the mystical energy that coursed throughout the universe. One by one, he attained mastery of the five remaining major siddhis: Tri-kāl-gyātvam, knowledge of the past, present and the future; Advandvam, tolerating extremes of temperature; Par-chitt abhigyān, the ability to read someone's mind; Pratistambhah, the power to modify the five elements; and the last and most important, Aparājyah or invincibility.

He was now immune to all trappings of the material world. No one could defeat him in a battle involving mystical powers and he already had control over physical ones since the yagnya he had organized all those years ago. Indra and his entourage would be hard-pressed to better him in case the situation arose.

After obtaining the major powers, he turned his attention towards the secondary siddhis that gave him control over hunger, thirst and cravings of the flesh, thereby making him immune to a repeat of the Menaka incident in future. He then attained enhanced visual and auditory capabilities so that he could see and hear from great distances.

His next acquisition gave him the ability to enter another person's body, while another made him a shape-shifter so that he could turn into any being—animal, bird, plant, Deva, Asur or Manav—he wanted. Yet another siddhi gave him the facility to communicate with the resident of any loka through telepathy. The last one, he realized, would come in really handy when he challenged the king of Devas himself.

After years of staying motionless and absorbing all these powers into his body, he finally turned his consciousness outwards and chanted a spell to dissolve the layers of mud covering his body, destroying the thousands of insects and their home instantly. He did not have time to think about anyone but his goal right now and any creature that came in his way would just be collateral damage.

He was now stronger than any human had been in the past and probably would ever be in the future. Finally, it seemed the universe was smiling on him and he would be able to fulfil his desire of defeating that arrogant son of Brahma.

The only wish he had now was an opportunity to humble his adversaries.

Adhyaye 32

The universe was indeed smiling upon Vishwamitra for, unknown to him, the fates had been conspiring to provide him the chance he was craving.

Through the long years that he had been lost in the infinite depths of Brahman power, time had moved on for the sovereign of Kosal, who had decided to withdraw from worldly affairs. The king considered himself too old to look after the kingdom and stepped down from the throne, anointing his son Harishchandra as his successor.

Satyavrat had been a just and devout ruler but now the idleness of his retirement was making him a little eccentric. He knew his Karma had been good and would quite possibly lead him to Swarg after he died, but his mind had somehow got stuck to the notion that he deserved to ascend to heaven in his own mortal body.

No one could shake him out of this fascination, for in his mind his logic was as sound as any logic could ever hope to be. This body was what had allowed him to accomplish all the good Karma in this life so how could he leave it behind in death?

To achieve his ambition, he had decided to take help of his designated preceptor, Brahmarishi Vasishth. The learned sage, who looked every bit the same as he had decades ago, gazed upon the king whose face was lined with wrinkles and whose thinning hair had turned completely white. The left eye was developing a cataract and the right knee had developed arthritis, yet he wished to take this body to the next realm because of his attachment to it.

He tried to explain to the king the transient nature of this world and said, 'Just as you or I change clothes when they get dirty, the soul changes its covering once it grows old and moves on to a brand-new body. What use do you have of such a body in the other world when it can't even sustain you properly in this one?'

Satyavrat tried to explain to the Brahmarishi the reason for his strange wish. 'Gurudev, I do not wish to take this body with me because of my attachment to it but for the sake of loyalty. The only way I could secure prosperity for my kingdom and my subjects was through this now-ailing body. How can I leave it here now and move on to the next realm? Wouldn't that be a kind of treachery on my part?'

The Brahmarishi addressed the king kindly, 'Rajan, what you say may seem logical to a layman but a learned king like yourself should not harbour such thoughts! Your argument shows your ignorance about your true nature; you identify yourself with the outer shell rather than the pearl that you actually are.

'Your body is made of the panch mahabhoot, the five basic elements of life, and if every person decides to take his or her body to the next world, the balance of these five elements would be affected. Besides, this is what the Srishti Karta has ordained and doing what you ask me to do would be meddling with the course of nature.'

Satyavrat felt disappointed but he did not let the Brahmarishi's refusal dishearten him and countered, 'How can I identify with something I have never seen, my lord? I know only of this body that has served me well throughout the vicissitudes of life and I cannot fathom an existence without it in the next world!'

Rishi Vasishth shook his head in vexation and said, 'My child, this body is but an extension of your soul! Tell me, when you refer to it as *your* body, who is the owner of the body that you refer to? When you call it *your* arm or leg, isn't it self-contradictory since all these parts form the entire *you*?'

He gave the old human some time to grasp the purport of what he had said before continuing. 'That *you* is the soul residing inside *your* body, which is but a vehicle for it to perform the functions of daily life. It is valuable here but completely redundant in the higher realms where your subtle body takes over these functions. It is futile for you to wish its continuation even after its utility is over.'

The king understood the logic of his argument but could not let go of his ambition. In this agitated state, he decided to approach the sons of Vasishth, for surely they, being of a younger generation, would understand his point of view better.

Shaktri, Vasishth's eldest son, was now a rishi in his own right and possessed enough powers to change the flow of nature, so Satyavrat went to him with folded hands. 'Rishivar, I have come seeking your help even as your great-souled father has turned me down. In the face of his reluctance, you are the next best alternative I have. Please do not disappoint me.'

Ever since the skirmish with Vishwamitra, Shaktri had detested kings. Satyavrat's strange request and his attempt to bypass Vasishth filled him with indignation. He looked at the old Kshatriya contemptuously and said with barely concealed anger, 'You dim-witted king, how dare you come to me when your own mentor has denounced you? If my father has declared it impossible, how can you ask me to conduct such a phantasmal ritual for you? Such a thought shouldn't even be entertained and a procedure to accomplish what you desire should never be performed!'

The king looked miserable and at some level Shaktri pitied him. How easy it was for these people, living in the lap of luxury, to get attached to the material objects around them, and desire to take them to the next world! He had heard of a kingdom in the west whose kings were busy building elaborate tombs for themselves, storing all their treasures inside as if they could carry them to Yamlok to bribe Yamraj into allowing them to enter Swarg! What a terrible waste it was since all that hoarded wealth could have been utilized for the welfare of their subjects. Some kings had even given orders to mummify their dead bodies to preserve them for the next world and this king in front of him seemed to be even one step ahead of them.

He shuddered at the level of the king's ignorance and said in a softer tone, 'Rajan, forget this childish whim and spend your last days in the worship of God. That is the only way you can attain heaven for the gross material bodies cannot survive in the ethereal realm of Swarglok. It is only our astral bodies that can adjust to the physical conditions of that world and you have no option but to leave this decaying form here itself.'

Satyavrat's confidence was shattered as he heard these words. When he had embarked on his journey, he had been hopeful of swaying the mind of his Brahmarishi Vasishth or at least his son because they were the only two people who had the spiritual power to perform such a feat in his knowledge.

Completely dejected, he said, 'I am so unfortunate that my last wish was rejected by both my kulguru as well as you, and I have now been reduced to the state of such opprobrium. However, I shall not rest till I have exhausted all my resources and will hunt for someone even better than you two!'

On hearing that, Shaktri became infuriated and cursed the old king, 'O muddle-brained Kshatriya, you think of your own desires so much and ignore the guidance of your mentors, hence you shall attain the state that you really deserve!

'You focus on fulfilling a meaningless craving, hence instead of the sacred fire of yagnya, you deserve to tend to the fire of a burning pyre. Instead of performing Vedic rituals you shall now live a life performing funeral rites for dead people. For this affront, I curse you to become a Chandal and be known as Trishanku for the three sins you have committed against your kingdom and your kulguru.'

Satyavrat fell at the feet of the sage who seemed to have lost all control over his anger. Tears fell from his eyes and he asked, sobbing, 'What sin have I committed, my lord, in asking for the fulfilment of a logical wish? Do I really deserve to be cursed thus?'

His argument made Shaktri angrier and he spluttered in rage. 'Do not forget the follies of your youth, my king! You may have lived a blemish-free life in recent times but how can you forget the grave injustices of your boyhood?'

Satyavrat stopped in the middle of saying something. His mind went back to the time when he had been appointed the king-in-waiting of Ayodhya. Drunk with the power his new position brought, he had abducted a Brahmin girl right from the wedding altar and fled with her. His father Tryaruni had banished him for a period of ten years for this act and he had spent those living a life of debauchery with his friends in the neighbouring kingdom.

He recalled another time when, overcome with hunger, he had killed the cow of a Brahmin and gorged on the meat of the holy animal that had supported the Brahmin's entire family. And now, he had gone against his mentor's advice, completing the three sins that Shaktri was now damning him for.

He did not have any heart to argue with the sage any more and Shaktri saw the dejection in his body language. He addressed the king for the last time and warned, 'If you do not desist from your foolish pursuit, you will spend all your remaining life trapped in a limbo from which you will never ever be able to escape.'

Adhyaye 33

Following the curse, Satyavrat's noble and kindly face turned ugly and dark. His rich clothes transformed into the rags worn by a Chandal and his silky white hair was replaced by shaggy dreadlocks. The fragrant garland around his neck turned into a funeral wreath and his body, now deformed, was smeared with crematory ash.

When he saw the changes that had come over him he howled in agony and limped from Shaktri's hermitage, shouting to the heavens. He knew he had done some unforgivable things in the past but he had more than made up for them throughout his kingship and did not deserve this grave injustice meted out to him. Reaching the market square, he wailed to his citizens but no help was forthcoming since no one recognized his altered form. He kept insisting that he was their former king, the one who had provided them all these riches, but they in turn just laughed at him, thinking he was a mad man caught in delusions of grandeur. A passing vaidya diagnosed his condition as mental psychosis and tried to take him to the hospital but he snarled at him in frustration and pushed him away.

If these people did not recognize him how would he ever gain entry into his own palace? The soldiers at the gates would definitely not let him pass and he would have to suffer more humiliation if his children also failed to identify him. Just this morning he had had everything—the comfort of his palace, the love of his family and the gratitude of his subjects—but it had all changed in just two prahers.

Struggling with his new deformities, he walked out of his kingdom and hobbled towards the jungle, hoping that a wild animal would kill him and put an end to his misery. He kept blaming the gods of fate for his condition, knowing not that destiny was leading him to the only man who would become the means of his salvation.

Fumbling through thorns and brambles, Satyavrat chanced upon the hermitage of Vishwamitra at the precise moment the rishi rose from his long penance.

As Vishwamitra opened his eyes and looked around, gradually adjusting to the sights, sounds and smells of the physical world, his gaze directly fell upon the madman who stood glaring at him as if he had seen a ghost. Rising from his samadhi for the first time in years, Vishwamitra divined the events that had transformed this king into an outcast and beckoned to him in sympathy.

Satyavrat's mind was still in turmoil and he did not know whether the apparition in front of him was a figment of his imagination or an actual person. Gradually his vision cleared and he realized the gaunt sage was gesturing to him to come closer.

He limped towards the spectre, knowing that there was no harm in doing so for he had nothing more to lose. To his surprise, as he neared the tall, regal-looking sadhu, he felt his pain disappearing and colour returning to his original form. Gone were the arthritis and his battle scars. Even his eyesight seemed improved! When he looked down at himself, he saw that his rags had changed back into regal finery.

He rubbed his now fully functional eyes to make sure this was not a trick his mind was playing on him and fell at the sage's feet in gratitude. Not only had Shaktri's curse been reversed, but his health had also been restored by this wonderful man.

Vishwamitra patted the king's head and asked him to get up, 'Utishth, Satyavrat,' he said, 'I have overturned the spell put on you and released you from its effects.'

The king was amazed that this man knew what had happened with him and asked, 'You know who I am, my lord?'

Vishwamitra nodded and said, 'I know the entire sequence of events that has led you to me, O king. And yes, I know the egotistical rishi putra who put the curse on you as well.'

Satyavrat felt hope rising in his heart; this man not only knew of his predicament but also did not think too highly of the Brahmarishi's son. Maybe he was the one who would help him fulfil his desire.

Vishwamitra read the thoughts coursing through the king's mind and said, 'I shall help you achieve your aspirations, Rajan, for I myself do not believe in the limitations set by Indra and his cronies regarding what a human being can or cannot attain in this mortal form.'

Satyavrat's voice trembled as he said, 'My lord, I do not know who you are, yet I believe every single word you say. I have propitiated the gods with various rituals and reigned over my subjects conscientiously. All my life, I have given alms to the needy and the obligatory appreciation to the gurus. Yet, when I asked for a boon, my mentors cursed me with such a deformity!' His voice choked with emotion and he took a pause to calm himself.

Then with folded hands he said to the rishi who had come like a messiah into his life, 'My lord, please know that if you help fulfil my last wish, I shall not have anything to repay you with. I have renounced my kingdom and have no claim to any property or riches that I can share with you. The only thing I possess is my body that you have so mercifully restored and I, Suryavanshi King Satyavrat, descendant of the great Ikshvaku himself, promise to remain your devoted servant all my life.'

Vishwamitra put his hands on the king's shoulders and spoke in a way that soothed the mind of the tormented king, 'Rajan, I do not require any servants nor do I wish to reduce someone of your stature to a mere page boy. I, Vishwamitra, the son of Kadhi and the erstwhile scion of Chandravansh, shall help you fulfil your ambition even if it means sacrificing all my yogic powers in return.'

Satyavrat's eyes split wide open for he had not realized till now who his benefactor was!

The legendary ruler of Mahodayapur who had obtained divine military technology and almost breached the boundaries of Kosal was now willing to act on his behalf, putting his hard-earned powers at stake. He prostrated himself on the ground, touching his head to the dust on the rishi's feet.

Vishwamitra made him rise and asked him to get ready for the biggest transformation of his life, realizing that this was the opportunity he had been waiting for all these years. His earlier encounter with Vasishth had been an impassioned act of revenge. This time, it would be a well-thought-out act of not just settling scores but exacting justice.

Adhyaye 34

Securing Satyavrat a position in heaven was easier said than done.

For starters, such an undertaking had never been attempted and there were no clues in the scriptures as to how it could be managed. Vishwamitra knew he would have to rely on his creativity and intuition and fabricate new spells to achieve this objective.

He knew Brahmarishis and their offspring sometimes travelled to Swarg but he had heard of no human ever going there before; except maybe Pururavas who was invited by Indra himself. The only way a human could reach heaven was if they earned enough good Karma, and that too after discarding these gross bodies.

He realized that he would first of all have to create a protective shell around the king so that his body was not damaged on its journey to heaven. The layer of protection would have to allow the king to breathe and perform other bodily functions normally as well as prevent him from burning up like a meteor in the atmosphere of Swarg at the time of entry.

From the in-depth knowledge he now had of the universe, he knew that sound was a form of energy and he planned to utilize the oscillations of pressure in the sound waves and convert them into an electric shield that would form a spacesuit for Satyavrat. But to achieve that conversion, he would need a transducer and, as he wandered around the ashram, he came upon the perfect choice.

The locals grew a lot of sugar cane at the edge of the forest and he realized that the sugar in them could act as the perfect piezoelectric substance!

Using his newly acquired magical skills, he managed to fashion his own personal Brahmadand from it. The memories of how the same instrument, in the hands of Vasishth, had defeated his Divya Astras haunted him, and he thought it only fitting that his own innovative gadget would help him balance the score now.

Besides creating a protective covering, he would also need a vehicle for Satyavrat's interstellar travel, like the Pushpak that Kuber used. The lord of the north, however, was a close associate of Indra and would never let him study the design of his vehicle. And he was not sure if the other space engineer he knew of, the Asur Maiy, would be of any help either. Widely recognized as the best viman maker in the three worlds, Maiy was after all an Asur, and both the Devas as well as his kind considered humans inferior and would never come to Satyavrat's aid.

What if he could provide the king his own siddhi that allowed him to travel between worlds? But that meant he himself would have to forsake it forever. No, he had to come up with some other alternative.

How about tapping a natural wormhole that existed between the solar system and the galactic centre? He knew a portal existed at the very centre of the Milky Way that connected to Swarg. If he could somehow utilize that, Satyavrat could reach Swarg using a hyperspatial jump within a matter of seconds.

Listing out the probable problems helped him find the potential solutions and, after thrashing out all possibilities, he began preparations for this never-tried-before ritual. He remembered that the Gayatri Mantra he had discovered could turn matter into energy and vice versa and knew that if he could but use it properly, he would be able to achieve his objective, however difficult it seemed right now.

While he meditated, formulating new mantras, Satyavrat diligently worked to make the hermitage fit enough to conduct a sacrifice. The king, who had never lifted a finger to even clean his own bed, began clearing the ashram of excessive vegetation and followed up by collecting sufficient amounts of offerings so that the ritual would not have to be interrupted midway.

They toiled in their own ways, bonded by a mutual wish to help each other and, after a few days, a sort of friendship sprang between the two. In the evenings, they would sit together over supper, the Suryavanshi king sharing his life story with the Chandravanshi hermit-king who in turn would tell him the tales from his own life.

Both their dynasties had begun in the faraway mists of time when Vaivasvat Manu, the eldest offspring of the sun god, had sired nine sons and a daughter. While his sons, including Satyavrat's ancestor Ikshvaku, had given rise to the solar dynasty, Manu's daughter Ila had proceeded to marry Budha, the son of the moon god, and given birth to the lunar dynasty.

Vishwamitra was the thirteenth in his lineage while Satyavrat was the twenty-seventh. They discussed this apparent mismatch between their generations and came to the conclusion that the Chandravansh must have begun much later than the Suryavansh.

To give him confidence, Vishwamitra decided to discuss his plans with Satyavrat, telling him exactly how he planned to execute this impossible feat and the king marvelled at the ingenuity of his new preceptor. He had revered Vasishth and his guidance throughout his kingship but now he had a feeling that this raj-rishi may well turn out to be even superior to the Brahmarishi in his spiritual accomplishments.

Vishwamitra had calculated astrological alignments to check the best possible time for the opening of the wormhole and he planned to start the yagnya twenty-four hours before that muhurat to make sure Satyavrat's protective gear was in place before he entered hyperspace.

On the appointed day, both of them took a dip in the Kaushiki, chanting prayers to Ganesh, the remover of obstacles, who was not a part of Indra's coterie. Vishwamitra knew the multitude of gods and goddesses residing in Swarg would never help him and hence he had warned the king not to waste any time remembering them. He realized, though, that the ritual still depended on one Deva, Agni, but trusted him not to defy Brahma's orders of being a friend to all species of life irrespective of his personal opinion about them. All this was, however, kept out of any outsider's vision by a veil of invisibility that Vishwamitra had spread around the ashram for he did not want the meddling Devas to send their minions to disrupt his procedure.

Their prayers completed, both of them stepped out of the water in the inky-blue darkness of predawn and came to sit beside the yagnya vedi that had been prepared earlier. The sacred fire was lit using arani wood and, as the sun rose upon the horizon, Vishwamitra poured the first offering to Shri Hari Vishnu, requesting His support in this endeavour, just as the lord had helped Brahma in the beginning of creation.

As the fire grew in intensity, both the participants began chanting verses for Shiva, the primeval purush whose union with Shakti had made possible the coming together of matter and energy in this universe. They then paid tribute to Brahma, the maker of all living beings including Manavs, Danavs and Devas, reminding the Creator that all of them were equally his progeny.

Once the holy trinity had been appeased, Vishwamitra prayed to Lakshmi, the goddess of fortune, to bless them with success; Kali, to remove all obstacles from his path; and finally Brahma's consort Saraswati, focusing on her aspect as Gayatri.

He thought of the goddess as his own personal discovery; out of the millions that populated this planet, she had chosen to become visible only to him. As the day progressed, he methodically kept fusing hymns he had borrowed from the Kalpa Sutra with the powerful Gayatri beej mantra, resulting in verses that were not mere words but powerful spells that possessed the power to alter physical reality.

The piezoelectric effect of these verses gave rise to crackling blue electrical energy on the Brahmadand and Vishwamitra kept diverting it towards Satyavrat's body, forming a high-voltage layer of protection around the king as he stood transfixed by the miracle that was unfolding in front of his eyes.

Even though it surrounded him completely, the electrical charge did not come in contact with the king's skin and he could move his limbs and breathe and speak without any restriction. The only limitation he faced was in ingesting a new substance into his body because the protective shield would not let any external substance, material or otherwise, affect his body.

Vishwamitra told him that his novel spacesuit would last for at least another twenty-four hours, which was enough time for him to enter the environs of Swarg and become accustomed to it. Thereafter, the energy of Swarg's sun would recharge it allowing it to keep renewing itself till such time as Satyavrat felt he could do without it.

The process went on for close to six prahers and Vishwamitra knew the time for opening the portal was close. He had managed to locate the wormhole that would help Satyavrat travel to Swarg within minutes, if not seconds, and he needed to tap into its opening at the opportune moment. The fact that he could also utilize the same sometime in the future did not escape him.

It was the last praher of night, yet the otherwise pitch-dark jungle glowed with a supernatural light. Satyavrat was bathed in his protective gear even though its intense light did not inconvenience him inside the shell. Hungry flames leapt to the sky while Vishwamitra kept pouring oblations, channelling Agni's energy into the creation of the portal through which Satyavrat would access the space tunnel.

His face glowed with the warmth of the sacred fire and shadows flickered around him as the flames changed shapes. As the auspicious muhurat approached, Vishwamitra signalled to the king to get ready and Satyavrat waited in anticipation.

Within seconds, the space behind him began to shimmer and an oblong, undulating doorway appeared in the emptiness. He gulped nervously and hoped the rishi knew what he was doing, for the alternative would either fry him in the heat of the sun or, worse still, freeze him in the coldness of outer space.

Vishwamitra's entire concentration was focused on keeping the portal open so he gestured with his hand for the king to enter as soon as possible. The king had come so far that he had no option but to trust his benefactor and believe in his capabilities. He bowed low to the rishi and, taking a deep breath, stepped into the doorway to the other world.

Finally the moment of reckoning had arrived.

Adhyaye 35

Satyavrat's body hurtled through a dark tunnel and it seemed to him that his very organs were being turned inside out.

Even though he knew, or rather believed, that his body would not be hurt in this process, yet he wasn't sure how his mind would react to it. It was one thing to know the theory of the principle but completely another to experience it first-hand.

What if Vishwamitra had miscalculated the distance or the route of the journey? He had a sinking feeling of not finding any object to grip in this weightlessness and getting lost in the surrounding vacuum. He prayed fervently to the holy trinity to save him from bumping into a passing asteroid or being incinerated within the core of a sun.

The journey to the galactic centre lasted half a muhurat but to Satyavrat it seemed like a lifetime had passed before he switched tunnels and then abruptly landed at the pearly gates of Amravati, the capital city of Swarg. He took stock of his surroundings and steadied himself. Because of the protective shield his body had remained completely unharmed and he could breathe properly even in this alien land. He looked at the huge glittering postern in front of him and noticed two very tall creatures guarding it.

As he approached the door, the creature on his left raised a hand to halt his progress. The king looked around and gradually became aware of the entire perimeter being guarded by more such beings. They had bodies similar to humans except for an extra pair of limbs sprouting from the midriff in each of which they held an intricate weapon. They wore black armour that glinted in the bright light of Swarg's two suns.

Swarg had two suns!

Satyavrat had never imagined it possible for two suns to bathe a planet with their light but now he knew how it looked. His energy shield protected him from the brilliance of their beams and he could see that one of them was reddish in appearance and gave off a warm radiance that gave Swarg its characteristic glow.

The creature was now face-to-face with the king even though it towered above him by more than two feet. Satyavrat did not know how to communicate with it. In some cultures people liked to hug or shake hands or nod in acknowledgement or bow from the waist but he knew of other cultures where such gestures were considered offensive.

Finally, he settled for a namaskar which was the least aggressive posture he knew and was least likely to be misconstrued for it involved no sudden thrusting forward of arms or baring of teeth or invading the other person's personal space. Apparently it worked, for the creature nodded in acknowledgement.

As the guard came closer, he got a feeling that he was being scanned from tip to toe and felt a little uncomfortable. Satyavrat hadn't thought much about what he would do or how he would approach things once he reached heaven and he realized he should have planned a little before coming here. The thought of reaching Swarg itself had seemed almost impossible and consumed most of his days, hence he had not even bothered to think about the finer details.

Now that he was here he had to improvise so he said to the guard with whatever confidence he could muster, 'I am Suryavanshi Satyavrat, the son of Tryaruni and the descendant of Ikshvaku. I am here to visit Indra, the king of the gods.'

The guard registered his response and nodded. After all guests were not unheard of in Swarg but it had not received any intimation of the arrival of this one. It had checked the antecedents of the guest with the database in its mind and it matched with the DNA of the person before it.

It said in a toneless voice, 'Greetings, king of Ayodhya. Your presence has been intimated to the royal court and someone should be here to welcome you shortly. May I request you to wait here till that time?'

Satyavrat felt relieved for his first exchange with a Swarg dweller, even if just a guard, had gone off smoothly. He nodded in agreement and was pointed towards another gate that seemed to have materialized on his left.

He entered the doorway gingerly, for the gravitational force here seemed stronger than Earth and he had to put in effort to lift his legs. As he slowly stepped inside, he saw a signboard telling him that he was in Nandanvana, Indra's fabled garden where wish-fulfilling trees grew. The air was crisp and fresh and the breeze carried the heady aroma of parijat flowers that he knew could grow only in the pure environment of heaven.

He spotted fountains of sparkling water and stooped to take a little water in his palm but, as soon as he touched it, his energy shield repelled the alien matter. Satyavrat realized his folly and desisted from touching anything else, strolling around the multicoloured trees that glittered with jewels and seemed to extend right up to Brahmalok.

He was marvelling at how high they seemed to have grown even in this enhanced gravity when his contemplation was disturbed by the sound of marching footsteps. He turned around and what he saw made his eyes pop out in panic.

A team of guards was walking towards him, their extended weapons clearly marking him as the target. Behind them walked a Deva even taller than them, looking both incredulous and angry at the same time.

Satyavrat had never imagined that the first Deva he would face in Swarg would be Indra himself, for he was more than sure that this being who marched determinedly towards him was none other than Shakra.

The scriptures described most celestials and he matched the portrayal of a red-faced angry young god with a superb physique and handsome features, dressed in fine clothing and accessories. And for confirmation Satyavrat needed to look no farther than at the weapon the being held in his right hand—it was the fabled Vajra!

This was the dreaded weapon that Shakra had used to kill Vritra, the terrible dragon who had siphoned off all water from Earth, forcing its creatures to die of thirst and famine. Shakra had bested the beast, destroying his ninety-nine fortresses, and earned the epithet of Purandar. Reaching the inner cavern, he had finally slain the mighty dragon using this weapon that was considered invincible and Satyavrat now dreaded his fate.

As the guards moved closer in a tight circle, Shakra glared at him scornfully. He paced around the king, still not believing that a human had managed to land in Swarg without his knowledge and permission!

He had stopped paying attention to Vishwamitra after Menaka's return and had taken the threats she had passed on as words spoken in anger. But now it seemed he had underestimated the mortal, for he had managed to transport another human to Swarg with just his own powers!

He would figure out how he managed to do it later but for now he had to teach this filthy human a lesson. He locked eyes with the king and said with barely concealed malice, 'How dare you step onto the sacred soil of my home?'

Seething with anger, he glared down at the old king and said, 'Your mentor may have managed to transport you to the gates of Amravati but he won't be able to facilitate your entry, for you are a thrice-sinned man whom even his own kulguru forsook in the end. I admire his effort that has caught me unawares but all his brilliance is a waste, for you shall not be allowed to stay here a moment longer.'

Immediately two of Indra's guards rushed at Satyavrat in order to apprehend the intruder but to their surprise they were repelled by his protective shield. Their brains registered their failed attempt, yet they rushed again to grab the intruder but to no avail.

Indra was shocked by what he saw; his celestial guards were being repelled by a human? This was unheard of!

He ordered his troops to use their blasters but all that firepower could not so much as cause a dent on the shield that now glimmered and reflected Shakra's own bewildered expression. The leader of demigods could not believe that an energy shield created by a mere human was fending off laser blasts and cursed himself for letting his attention deviate from Vishwamitra.

He knew he could not let the humans gain this victory, else he would become the laughing stock of Swarg. He ordered his guards to step away and pointed his vajra at the human, using all its powers to toss him off Swarg.

His efforts started showing results and Satyavrat began to rise in the air. Shakra's face contorted with the exertion and he snarled at the king, 'I may not be allowed to wipe your puny frame off the face of this planet but can definitely push you off its surface. Shameless intruder, be prepared to be punished for trespassing as I throw you back to Earth. Your energy shield may have protected you from my weapons but let's see whether it can also protect you from the impact of crashing into your own planet!'

For the first time since emerging from the tunnel, the king felt really afraid for his life. He had been relieved that the shield had sheltered him from the laser shots but now it seemed even that wouldn't help. With a swishing sound he was flung out of Swarg and thrown into oblivion.

Adhyaye 36

Vishwamitra had followed the king's progress using his mystical powers and, as Shakra pushed him off his domain, the rishi rose to break his fall.

Raising his arms towards the skies, he began chanting mantras that would halt Satyavrat's descent. Invoking verses that could halt the motion of even bigger planets, he hoped they would work on the king's comparatively tiny frame and prevent him from crashing to his death.

He could now discern the approaching form of the king and breathed a sigh of relief when he saw his efforts being rewarded as the small projectile seemed to hover and come to an abrupt stop in the vast murkiness of space. He magnified his vision and was comforted to find the king alive and safe, still protected by the energy shield, though he was turned upside down. He had been falling head first for a while and all the blood had pooled in his head, turning his face red. He seemed to be shouting Vishwamitra's name though it wouldn't help since sound did not carry in vacuum.

Vishwamitra immediately established a mental connect with the distraught king and said, 'Do not worry! You have taken refuge with me and I shall not let you fall down to death.'

Satyavrat's expression seemed to change on hearing the rishi's voice and he seemed to get a grip on himself. Vishwamitra fumed at the disrespect shown to his protégé just because he was a human and therefore deemed unworthy of even stepping on the soil of heaven.

Turning the king upright, he spoke to Indra using his powers of telepathy, 'O arrogant son of Aditi, you have tried to thwart my penance and even succeeded in disrupting my efforts once but today, the man who stands in front of you is much stronger than the one you defeated earlier! How dare you show such disrespect to a king who deserves to be in heaven by your own rules?'

Indra watched in angry disbelief as the descent of the Manav he had thrown out of Swarg stalled. He gnashed his teeth and replied in an equally threatening tone, 'O insolent human, who are you to question what I do in my kingdom? Whether this human deserves to reach heaven or hell shall be decided by Yamraj after his death, not by you.'

He knew his logic was right so he pressed on, 'How dare you both try to breach the sanctity of Swarg? I shall never let you or him break into my palace, you ungracious human. Do not forget that I possess the power to turn you and this ant into ash in a flash, just as my soldiers had turned your men into dust once!'

The moment he was reminded of the humiliation he had faced, a steely determination came over Vishwamitra's mind and he said, 'If that is the course you wish to take, be prepared for the consequences, O arrogant Deva. This man is destined for Swarg and I am sure even you have sufficient powers to be aware of this as well. You reject him now only because he refuses to pander to your whims like your courtiers and fan your ego to gain your favour.

'The Srishti Karta has not barred humans from travelling to other lokas, yet you and your minions guard Swarg as if it is your own ancestral property. To shatter your pride and show you what a mere human can achieve, I shall create a new heaven to rival your own this very instant!'

Shakra smirked at this statement and passed it off as a bluff. Surely this human could not have gathered so much power that he could create a completely new planet. Even he, Indra, could not do this, for this was a feat that could be achieved only by the Srishti Karta!

Within moments, however, his opinion changed as he watched with unblinking eyes a new star system beginning to emerge where that blasted Trishanku was hanging in the sky. What took zillions of solar years to form was taking shape right in front of him, within minutes!

A giant nebula emerged in the vast emptiness of space and quickly divided into a dense central mass and a peripheral portion that slowly began revolving around the nucleus. The central portion began turning into a non-compressible core that would form the seed for the germination of a star. The surrounding clumps of gas spread near its equatorial plane, forming a disc even as the core started to burst into life by fusing smaller molecules into larger ones. Interstellar dust began to aggregate in the disc, giving rise to small planet-like bodies that gradually gained mass and absorbed all floating debris into themselves.

Shakra watched in disbelief as an entire solar system was formed in front of his eyes within a muhurat! He could not believe that Vishwamitra was going to prove him wrong right in front of his very eyes.

In his panic, the only solution that came to his mind was to take help from the Creator since only he could stop this madman from disturbing the equilibrium of the universe.

By the time Brahma appeared at the scene, Vishwamitra's planets were done and he was busy populating them with different species of life. His eight eyes watched the new planetary system in amazement, appreciating the way Vishwamitra had taken care of every factor.

There were three planets in the new solar system, all habitable owing to a proper distance from the sun, and each had land as well as oceans to support all forms of life. The third planet was enveloped by a thick atmosphere that could even support large avian beings and, for all practical purposes, this seemed the primary focus of his attention. The Srishti Karta was both baffled and impressed at this prodigious feat for he himself had required guidance to begin the process of creation.

Even as the two divine beings watched, one in admiration, the other in dismay, three more star systems had come up, each with their own planets. Life was emerging in its varied hues with humanoids developing from primates and their precursors. Eons of evolutionary process was being fast-forwarded to give rise to a kingdom for Vishwamitra's disciple!

The Srishti Karta smiled inwardly at India's discomfort in the face of this phenomenal display of power; he knew the leader of gods had not acted properly.

He took a deep breath and motioned for Indra to stay calm. It was time for him to intervene.

Adhyaye 37

Vishwamitra was thrilled!

It was true that he had assembled as many metaphysical powers as any human could and was the master of twenty-three siddhis, yet he had never imagined the extent to which he could modify his environment using them.

So engrossed was he in his endeavour that he failed to notice the blast of blue light that emerged right in front of him. It wasn't until the Srishti Karta addressed him that he realized he was in the presence of the Creator Himself.

'Vishwarath,' Brahma dev said in a voice that was like the booming of thunder.

The hermit-king paused in the middle of creating the royal palace and, bowing to the Creator, exclaimed, 'I can't believe I have been blessed with the presence of the Srishti Karta Himself! Many salutations to you, Lord Hiranyagarbha!'

Brahma's six eyes critically appraised the human who had managed to rival his own work so beautifully. He raised the front right arm in blessing and said in the same thundering voice, 'This is indeed a remarkable feat you have accomplished, O Manav.

'Never before in the history of this universe has a descendant of Manu managed to accomplish such an extraordinary feat.

You have achieved what even the finest architects of the Devas and Asurs cannot dream of and for good reason, for such an exercise can upset the critical balance of the entire universe!'

Thinking that the Creator was unhappy with his actions, Vishwamitra fell down on his knees and said with emotion, 'Forgive me, World Father, if I have offended you in any way, for this display of creativity was not meant as an affront to You but as a lesson in humility to the arrogant Devas. I am but a servant of the Supreme Brahman and not even worth a grain of dust on your holy feet!'

Brahma smiled and said, 'I wasn't unhappy when you managed to extract the Gayatri Mantra from the very heart of Surya, earning the sobriquet of Vishwamitra, and I am certainly not unhappy with your remarkable achievement today. Rather, it fills my heart with great pride that one of my own creations has managed to surpass even me in creativity.'

Vishwamitra was surprised; this was the first time in his long career that he had been praised by anyone for breaking the rules that had been set for him!

The Srishti Karta continued with his praise, overwhelming him with emotion, 'You have shown the world that a human, however small or insignificant he may seem, retains within his heart the power to break the limitations of his physical form. From this point onwards, anything created synthetically, cloned from something that exists naturally, shall be called "Vishwamitra's Srishti" in your honour.'

'However,' Brahma dev continued, 'if any creature tries to duplicate my own creation, it can lead to a breakdown of the system and result in a state where there are no rules and, instead of the regulations I have set, each person's will stands paramount. The balance between fate and free-will is a delicate one and I do not wish for that to be upset so radically.'

Vishwamitra's heart skipped a beat. Was the Srishti Karta going to demolish his creation? He would be well within his rights to do that, for such a creation could be dangerous for Swarg and the Devas who were related to him by family ties!

But Brahma sensed his thoughts and said, 'Your human thoughts are amusing to sift through. The tiniest of living organisms in this vast universe is related to me the same way the Devas ruling them are. There is a reason why it is known as the Brahmaand! To ensure such a feat is not repeated, I shall have to put a stop to your efforts. But the planetary systems you have created shall not be destroyed and shall keep functioning outside the purview of Shakra and other Devas.'

The hermit-king could not believe his ears as the thundering voice continued to speak, 'The parallel heavens you have created shall continue to be inhabited by the life forms you have populated them with. Satyavrat shall be their master, living there in his own mortal body that shall forever be protected by the self-sustaining shield you have covered it with.'

Vishwamitra glanced towards where Satyavrat had been hanging and saw the shield glowing with the radiance of a star. The right face of Brahma followed his gaze and his raised hand gestured in the air, taking the hanging human into the palace created for him. This magnanimous signal put the stamp of approval on Vishwamitra's creation and he knew no one would dare touch it again.

Brahma's central face looked kindly at him and said, 'Your astounding achievement shall be remembered for all eternity by the residents of Earth and these new solar systems shall remain visible in the southern hemisphere as the Crux. They will serve the purpose of guiding humans just like the North Star and Big Dipper do for those living in the northern hemisphere.

'Furthermore, since you have acted on the conviction that every creature deserves to achieve the highest of platforms in this universe, I hereby declare that no living being shall be barred from the higher lokas on the mere whim of a higher being. For your efforts, which have great ramifications for all of mankind, I confer on you the title of Maharishi.'

Vishwamitra barely managed to control the tears that were stinging at the corner of his eyes. This was more than what he had ever hoped for. He silently blessed Satyavrat for becoming the means for avenging his earlier humiliation and bringing him this breakthrough.

He had won the battle against the Devas and had shown them their correct place in the hierarchy of things. From now on, no man would consider himself inferior to a Deva just because he or she was born on Earth and would be capable of achieving the highest honours if he just put his heart into it.

Adhyaye 38

Indra returned to Swarg with a heavy heart. To be defeated by a human!

The fact that the same human had been subjected to humiliation by his forces earlier did not seem to matter. He had acted then in the interests of safeguarding his resources and in his mind it was a completely justified act.

Besides, the episode with Menaka had not just hurt Vishwamitra but Shakra himself for, after returning from Earth, the Apsara had requested that she be permanently relieved from her duties. The task had taken too much out of her and he had let her go with a heavy heart. He pitied her condition but knew it had been a necessary sacrifice to safeguard the happiness of Swarg for a human could never be allowed to rule the heavens.

As he thought about the events that had transpired, he admitted to himself that the Srishti Karta had acted quite impartially.

Shakra recognized greatness when he saw it. Vishwamitra's accomplishment was nothing short of a coup and he deserved to have a heaven for himself but who knew whether that would satiate his ambition or further drive him towards claiming sovereignty over Swarg as well?

He knew this subject would have to be debated with all parties involved and summoned a meeting of the council of thirty-three Devas.

The Trayastrimsa Council, as it was called, consisted of the twelve Adityas that included Shakra himself and his younger brothers Ansh, Aryaman, Bhag, Daksh, Mitra, Pushan, Savitra, Surya, Vishwakarma, Vaman, Varun; eight Vasus or the elemental gods comprising Agni, Antariksh, Apa, Chandra, Dhara, Dyaus, Nakshatra, Vayu; and eleven Rudras who were the three-eyed fierce manifestations of Lord Shiva.

The two remaining positions had earlier belonged to Prajapati Brahma and Shri Hari Vishnu but it was difficult to get them to join, hence the Ashwins, the twin sons of Surya, had been added to the council. The usual protocol was for them to have a meeting and, convey their conclusion to the Srishti Karta for approval and in case he gave his nod, the proposal would go for Shri Hari Vishnu's consideration. Not that Shakra wanted this to go to the highest level for deliberation, for he could never be sure which way Shri Hari Vishnu's vote would swing as the lord was fair to a fault!

No doubt His Avatars had saved the Devas many a times from the atrocities committed by Asurs, yet he had also supported the latter in some instances and had a soft corner for the Manavs. No, they would have to figure this out themselves, making sure their future actions remained below the radar.

The council met in the hexagonal court where the Adityas were led by Shakra while Chandra led the Vasus. The Rudras were represented by Shambhu who was considered the closest to Lord Shiva and whatever he said held a lot of weight.

Addressing the gathering, Shakra opened the proceedings, 'Dear congregation, it is with a thoughtful heart that I address you today. Recent events must have come to your notice as well and by now perhaps the entire sentient universe knows of the creation of four more star systems by no more than a human!'

There were murmurs and nods of assent and he continued, 'What you may not know, however, is that these stars and their planetary systems have been ordained to forever remain out of the purview of the thirty-three gods.'

The assembly broke into an uproar at this. How could that be? Weren't the Devas supposed to be overlords of all that existed above Earth?

Shakra let them build up their anger and when he felt they were ready, he spoke his next words, 'The question we have to ask ourselves is: Should we let that happen?'

Cries of denial rose from all sections and Shakra nodded in satisfaction. He needed to fuel their indignation and use it to his advantage, for he needed their help to teach a lesson to the human in such a way that no one could implicate him in the future.

He raised a hand to silence them and said, 'But we are bound by the diktat given by the Srishti Karta; how can we go against Pra-pitamah's orders?'

He deliberately used the honorific to stress that he was the great-grandson of Brahma and hence bound to his orders through family ties. He looked at the leader of the Vasus for his estimation of the situation, for they were both bound to the Creator by the same relation.

Predictably enough, Chandra was cautious in his approach. 'I condemn this misuse of the elements by someone who is not designated by the Supreme Lord to perform such a function. Yet, I admire the efforts of this man . . . '

Shakra cut him off mid-sentence, knowing well that Chandra's view could tilt the opinion for or against what he had in mind and said, 'Well said, Chandra, we know it is a difficult position for you to take, for the concerned man belongs to your own lineage, yet you show solidarity with the brotherhood and we respect you for that.'

Everyone nodded, sharing words of sympathy, and Shakra knew that, by saying this, he had put an end to whatever support Chandra may have intended to give Vishwamitra's efforts. He looked towards Varun and Vayu, silently nudging them for support.

Vayu was a Vasu as well so he pitched in first. 'I completely agree with the assessment of our leader Chandra; such an abuse of the panch mahabhoot as displayed by this Chandravanshi is not acceptable.'

Shakra smiled for he knew his friend had purposefully used the dynastic terminology to further stress the indirect responsibility of Chandra in the affair. Looking around, he observed with satisfaction that the general sentiment of the assembly was with him.

However, Mitra, the patron god of friendship, had a different of opinion. 'Do we have to take this as an act of aggression? Why don't we just shake hands and sign a pact with this Manav to show our appreciation of his prodigious achievement? We have many worlds to take care of; what difference does it make if this man looks after a few more which, by the way, were never under our domain to begin with?'

Varun countered this argument by saying, 'No, my soft-hearted friend, we cannot let anyone, least of all this human, get away with what you have rightly proclaimed a prodigious achievement. Imagine what would happen if he continues to do so in the future and tomorrow ends up cloning even us Devas to run this creation of his. What would be our position in the hierarchy of this universe if such a situation were to present itself?'

This was a new thought and everyone sat pondering it. Shakra took the opportunity to prod Surya. 'What does my youngest brother think of this situation? You ought to have some opinion about it since it is a Suryavanshi who started this whole mess!'

Surya looked at his eldest brother and nodded meekly. 'I know, jyesth, that even as Vishwamitra is putting Chandra into a dock, my descendant Satyavrat is equally to blame. I do not agree with his actions, however, and give you my unconditional support.'

Shakra gave him a curt nod; after all in case of a confrontation, it was imperative he had the support of his own family before he relied on the other factions. He then looked towards the leader of Rudras and asked, 'Does my dear friend Shambhu have anything to add to the discussion?'

The chief Rudra was built like a wrestler and did not like to talk much. In most such meetings, he sat brooding and gave his opinion only at the end of the discussion.

On being asked a direct question, he regarded Shakra with his three eyes and answered, 'I believe the current situation has come to pass not only because of the unfulfilled ambitions of these Manavs but also because of the misreading and mishandling of it in the initial stages by our lord.'

Shakra felt himself turn red with embarrassment but he knew someone was bound to raise this point at some point of time, so the sooner he got it out of the way, the better it was.

To diffuse the negative emotions he said, 'I agree, I may have reacted prematurely but the very act that we sit discussing today more than vindicates the actions taken by me. If I had not done what I did then, who knows, we may have had to confront this man's audacity much earlier!'

He looked directly in the eyes of Shambhu who kept looking right back. After a while the impasse broke and the Rudra conceded gracefully, 'Possible . . . '

Shakra was relieved that he had avoided a stalemate with the hulk by owning up to his impulsive actions, for he knew how difficult it would be to get Shambhu to change his stand once he took one. Aloud he said, 'So we all stand unified in our reading of the situation that it is dangerous for our future. Now the question arises as to what can be done to mitigate this danger?'

When no resolution was offered, he said, 'If no one has a concrete solution, I offer to present in front of the council a means to regain our lost prestige.' He was careful not to sound too presumptuous and self-indulgent and it seemed to work because he got murmurs of encouragement from the gathering.

Looking at the leader of the Vasus, he said, 'Since the current situation has been created by one of your descendants, the prime responsibility for its correction lies on your shoulders. You cause the sap to flow in plants and the blood and lymph in animals to ensure their nourishment. You are the master of all fluids running through the organisms on Earth. Just as you cause the tides in Earth's oceans, I suggest you bring about a turmoil in Vishwamitra's mind and make him do things he otherwise may not do given the recent growth in his spiritual quotient.'

Chandra looked at Indra's determined face and knew what he was being asked to do. He had to turn Vishwamitra's inner calm into the madness that a werewolf felt at the time of the full moon. In short, from a maharishi working on reason, he had to turn him back into a savage driven by instinct.

When he nodded his acceptance, Shakra turned his attention towards the Rudra and said, 'My friend, you are the personification of turmoil and destruction. I want you to fill this man's soul with an insatiable quest for revenge. Churn his heart even as you churn the winds in a tornado to bring about Devastation at the end of a yuga.'

The leader of Rudras merely grunted in reply and Shakra then glanced at his own brothers, focusing his attention on

Surya. 'You, my anuj, are the lord of the intellect so I entrust you with the responsibility of ensuring that the heightened emotions and the boiling blood of this man lead him towards but one direction—Brahmarishi Vasishth—for that is where the solution to all our problems lies.'

Adhyaye 39

The encounter with the Srishti Karta had brought great peace to Vishwamitra's heart, for he knew now that all the efforts he had made in his life for advancing on the path of spirituality had been finally rewarded.

Yet, strangely enough, there was one hankering that he could not seem to get rid of.

Even with all that he had gained, he could somehow not forget the condescending way Vasishth had talked to him all those years ago in the foothills of the Himalayas. He had been a broken man that day and the pain he had felt in his heart still stoked his anger.

He wanted the Brahmarishi to acknowledge him as an equal and give him the respect he deserved, for now it was Vasishth's own father, the Srishti Karta, who had declared him a Maharishi. Maybe he should confront the arrogant Vasishth and demand this approval.

As this thought overrode everything else on his mind, Vishwamitra marched towards the Brahmarishi's ashram, having located it by using his powers. With the speed of thought he reached the hermitage that stood right outside the woods surrounding Ayodhya. But as he appeared behind a giant kadamb, he heard loud voices coming from the direction of the ashram and decided to watch the unfolding events from his vantage point behind the tree.

A Brahmin and a king were arguing in the middle of the tiny wooded path with both claiming the right to pass first. He recognized the Brahmin to be Shaktri, the eldest son of his arch rival who had dared to first challenge him when he had approached Nandini!

He had missed the first part of the argument but he could figure what had happened. The king was on a horse followed by his soldiers in a single file since the clearing in the dense forest was narrow. Shaktri and his younger brothers, who had also grown by now, had been walking in a single file as well. Now the question was which group should step aside to let the other one pass first.

The king had called out to Shaktri to move out of his way but the Brahmin had replied arrogantly, 'King Kalmashpad, I am a Brahmin which is the highest caste in the society and you know that even a king must give way to a Brahmin. The path is mine to traverse first and I would like you and your men to make room for us to pass.'

The king laughed scornfully and said, 'You scrawny forest dweller, how dare you compare yourself to a king like me. This region of the forest is in my domain and my will rules supreme here. Leave the path and run away to your little huts, else I shall show you who the true master here is!'

Vishwamitra saw Shaktri turn red with anger and shout insults at the king, calling him a brute barbarian. He was reminded of his own skirmish with Vasishth and felt the old rage rise again. Apparently, this man's vanity and pride had only grown in all these years and he was still unable to control his baser instincts.

Vishwamitra had been accused of high-handedness by this

rishi putra then, and he wanted to see how the king in front of him would react. He knew no self-respecting king would take such words lying down and, sure enough, the furious Kalmashpad lashed out at Shaktri with his whip!

The lash hit Shaktri right on the chest and he reeled under the impact. His brothers helped him regain balance and he rose sputtering like an angry cobra.

With a hand full of sanctified water, he pronounced a terrible curse on the king. 'You prove my words true by behaving like an early cave-dwelling human! Oh brute savage, may you lose your position and turn into an ogre right this instant!'

Vishwamitra was stunned by the ease with which this Brahmin had uttered such a terrible curse on a fellow human! Brahmins were supposed to look after the spiritual growth of the entire society and help other castes progress with the help of their knowledge, yet this one seemed too full of pride to do justice to his position. He remembered belatedly that this was the same man who had cursed Satyavrat as well and deformed his body into that of a Trishanku. Even as his mind processed these thoughts, he saw a transformation begin in the king.

Kalmashpad's body was growing in size and his clothes and jewellery started popping off his torso. The horse he was riding could not take his weight any more and collapsed and he was thrown off its back. His soldiers watched with fear the change taking place in their king and took several steps back.

His skin was changing colour and it seemed to be bubbling and breaking out in boils. A stench rose from the man and the Brahmins covered their noses in disgust. His hair fell off and teeth and nails grew in size to resemble fangs and claws while horns sprouted from his head.

Even Vishwarath felt a tinge of fear, watching a man turn into an ogre by the power of a Brahmin's curse. What an impact some sanctified water and few mantras could achieve! He felt disgusted by the pain this rishi was inflicting on a fellow human. It was because of people like him that human beings remained trapped in such petty infighting instead of setting their goals on higher pursuits.

To his amazement, even with all the changes happening in the king's body, he did not seem to have lost any of his previous anger. Kalmashpad saw his transformed body and growled like a wild animal. Vishwamitra realized this was the perfect opportunity for him to avenge his insult!

Summoning his own powers, he infused the now growling ogre with the spirit of a man-eating rakshas, urging him to do what came to him naturally. The ogre lunged forward and grabbed the man closest to him—Shaktri!—and, pulling him to his mouth, he broke his head with one snap of his jaw!

Shaktri would never have imagined his curse would rebound on him so badly. He did not even get the time to register the irony of the situation as his body dropped to the ground, spilling blood into the lush green vegetation.

The other Brahmins tried running away but Kalmashpad grabbed them and one by one snapped each of their necks, biting their heads off and drinking their blood. His own men were lucky enough to be on horses so they rode away as fast as they could while the ogre himself ran towards the ashram of Vasishth.

Vishwamitra realized that if the monster attacked Vasishth, his own objective would remain unfulfilled. Maybe he should have tried to save the rishi's other sons as well, for after all the rest of them had been innocent. Shaktri's hubris had brought this on him but the others could have been spared.

Then his blood started to boil again remembering the slight he had endured at the hands of these Brahmins. They were the reason he had lost his special troop of hundred soldiers that had been turned into ash. No, it was better this way. This would be his revenge for Vasishth's destruction of the soldiers he had nurtured like sons.

He could now confront Vasishth without having to bother about his pesky sons and he proceeded to intercept the ogre and then deal with his arch-enemy once and for all. He managed to stop the creature just as he was about to reach Vasishth's ashram and deflected his path so that he would keep running around the hermitage without ever finding the Brahmarishi's hut. That would give Vishwamitra some time to decide how he wanted to deal with this nuisance.

As he himself reached the precinct, he saw a young woman sitting outside with a baby in her lap. His yogic vision told him it was the widow of Shaktri and the child in her hand was the infant Parashar. He was feeling magnanimous so did not harm them. After all, Vasishth's entire clan had already been wiped out and with the immense powers he possessed now, the small kid could hardly do him any harm in the future.

He approached the mother–son duo and requested an audience with Vasishth. Oblivious to the fate that had befallen her husband, the woman rose respectfully and informed him that the rishi had retired permanently to the Himalayas with his wife, to his erstwhile ashram. Apparently, the fall of his mentee Satyavrat had shaken his belief in humans and he had decided to distance himself from the affairs of men once again.

Giving them a grateful smile, he marched towards the Great White Mountains. The irony of the location was not lost on him, for that was the very spot where it had all begun.

Adhyaye 40

Once again he was back in the woods that he had loved as a boy. He admired the sylvan surroundings and the towering conifers that gave off a heady fragrance. Sunlight barely managed to filter through the thick branches and the grass was littered with bursting pine cones.

He walked slowly towards Vasishth's ashram with the intention of destroying his nemesis once and for all, remembering all the events that had transpired here. His stumbling upon the strange bonhomie between predators and their prey, his exploration of the confines of the ashram, his welcome by Vasishth's young sons and his subsequent introduction to the Brahmarishi, the sumptuous meal he and his men had savoured at this very place and his astonishment at meeting the divine provider of that feast.

All those were good reminiscences but the events that had followed had soured those memories. As he moved towards the sole hut that remained there, he got a glimpse of the enclosure where he had met Nandini. He wondered where the magical being was now and once again his heart filled with a desire to obtain her.

His mind was thrown back to the physical and mental trauma that he endured at the hands of the SOS, the annihilation of his best soldiers after a hard-earned victory and his dejected return to Kanyakubja.

There had been a brief period of exhilaration when he had conducted the great yagnya that gave him access to the Divya Astras but that was also short-lived as those weapons were swallowed by a small wooden staff held boldly aloft by an old rishi. And perhaps the most hurtful was the sermon he had received from Vasishth as if he was a schoolboy!

He would avenge his insult today and settle the score decisively and with this confidence, he kept moving ahead towards the small dwelling. As he came closer, his sharp ears caught sounds that he could identify as those of the Brahmarishi and his wife. His mind had become so muddled with thoughts of revenge that he could only imagine them plotting against him for surely Vasishth must have learnt of the demise of his sons through his yogic powers by now.

His blood boiled like a churning cauldron and his heartbeat intensified as he realized that the moment he had been waiting for was upon him.

Should he take the Brahmarishi by surprise and just blast him into oblivion? No, he had just finished creating a completely new star system and was powerful enough to take on the might of the Brahmarishi.

He pondered over the best way to bring about Vasishth's annihilation—should he drown him in a river or throw him into an active volcano? Pierce him with a thousand pieces of glass or burn him slowly in a vat of oil? No need for Yama's men, he could show Vasishth his own personal vision of hell.

His paranoia stoked by the combined efforts of the plotting Devas, told him that the two were planning to kill him right now and, on a sudden whim, he decided to hear what the two were talking about before proceeding to wipe them off the face of Earth.

Arundhati, Vasishth's wife, was sobbing while the old rishi was trying to console her. 'Do not weep, my dear, for death is only a means to attain the next level of spiritual growth. You know as well as I do, or perhaps even better, that Shaktri had been letting his passions rule over reason for quite some time now.

'Even the birth of a child, which generates feelings of love in the hardest of hearts, failed to rid him of his anger. He was also a bad influence on our other sons and, in the time to come, this could have turned into a bigger problem. Vishwamitra's act has only served to free all of them from a doomed future.'

Vishwamitra was perplexed. Had the old Brahmarishi turned soft in his advancing age?

To his surprise the woman seemed to accept this explanation and replied in a measured tone, 'I know how this cycle of birth and death works, my lord, but it takes time for the heart to accept what the mind already knows. Even though we realize the futility of clinging to other mortals, yet the attachment to one's family is too strong for their loss not to affect us.'

Vasishth nodded in understanding and gently stroked her head. Then she asked her husband, 'Is it true that the man who brought about the demise of our sons has been conferred with the title of Maharishi by none other than the Srishti Karta himself?'

'Yes, my dear,' Vasishth said, 'and it gives me pride to acknowledge the role I have been able to play in his development!'

Vishwamitra could not believe his ears when he heard the reply but the Brahmarishi continued, 'The day I met him, I knew this man was going to achieve what no one had managed to before him. He had the blessings of Ruchik, the guidance of Dattatreya and the intellect of Kadhi and whatever I have done since that moment was to nudge him in a way that would lead him towards his final destination.'

Vishwamitra was stunned. This being, whom he had always thought of as his sworn mortal enemy, had actually been guiding his progress all along?

He remembered what the Brahmarishi had said when he had first argued for possession of the divine cow—'Nandini is not a property of this ashram and lives here of her own volition. We have no more the right to let her go than one could let go of a person of their own family.'

He had then been teaching him about letting go of his desire to appropriate material wealth. The learned sage had told him in so many words that nothing in this world belonged to anyone except the Supreme God Himself. Each creature had His permission to live the life the way he wanted to. Subconsciously, Vishwamitra realized, this was the very thought that had pushed him into finding his own destiny!

The Brahmarishi had not lifted a finger to hurt him even though he could easily have defeated his army single-handedly. He had taken it as a personal attack by Vasishth but it was Nandini's reluctance and his own pride that had brought about the annihilation of his forces.

Even when he had confronted him the second time, the Brahmarishi had only thwarted his missiles and not attacked him in retaliation. He recalled the verses recited to him when his Divya Astras had proven futile. '*Digh-balam shastra-balam, Bramha-tejo sarvocch balam*', reminding the king that the power of material arms, even of divine origin, was useless against the spiritual power obtained through penance.

It was this crushing defeat that had led him on the journey of self-discovery. Had he not been pushed into a corner, he would never have attempted anything other than becoming a universal monarch and could not have achieved the remarkable feats he had managed to. The sudden realization that it was Vasishth's refusal to help Satyavrat that led the king to Vishwamitra and seek his help hit him hard. Had the Brahmarishi fulfilled the king's ambition, and he was more than capable of doing it, Vishwamitra would never have got the opportunity to settle his score with Indra and show his prowess to the world!

In a sudden epiphany, he realized that Vasishth was the sole reason he had risen so far in his spiritual undertaking. He rushed inside to fall down at the feet of his absentee mentor, his heart full of repentance.

Arundhati recoiled in horror, seeing the murderer of her children in front of her, but Vasishth bent down to raise him by his shoulders and embraced him like a son. 'Today, my child,' he said 'you have surpassed all your previous achievements for the triumph over one's own desires is the biggest victory in this world.'

As Vishwamitra struggled to gain control over his emotions the Brahmarishi smiled at the remorseful man in front of him and said, 'Your journey has been of great loss and even bigger gains, yet this is the biggest accomplishment of them all. With each step you have strived to break the boundaries set for you and achieved what no one before you could even dream of.

'I am more proud of you than I have been of any of my sons and recognizing your spiritual advancement, I, Vasishth, the son of Srishti Karta Brahma Himself, hereby pronounce you a Brahmarishi!'

Vishwamitra had no words left to respond. As anger and despair flowed out of his eyes, he felt as if he was suddenly free from all desires.

He had vowed never to forget the humiliation Vasishth had put him through but now he knew it was the greatest benediction he could have received. His eyes still moist, he bowed to the Brahmarishi and his wife with folded hands, silently begging forgiveness for his role in the death of their sons and accepting the title that he had craved all his life from the man he had hated most of his life!

He had managed to gain control over the primeval emotions of lust, anger, pride, attachment and greed but could not become a Brahmarishi till he mastered the last and the most important—jealousy, for he now understood that as long as that emotion remained inside a man's heart, the other five could gain entry anytime.

He had dared to challenge the gods and even defeated them in some sense but his greatest achievement was his victory over his own heart. His destiny had never been to become the emperor of the world or a jeet-indra but to turn into the master of the senses, a jeet-indriya.

As the purpose of his life became clear, he felt a great burden lift off his shoulders. He finally understood that Man's ultimate destiny was to become the master of his own destiny. And man's destiny did not lay in just creating or obtaining material wonders but also in realizing his full spiritual potential.

He would share his knowledge and endeavour to advance mankind to become heirs to the gods. Whatever the future held, he would not rest till he had achieved this goal and truly become Vishwa-mitra—the friend of the world.

Epilogue

He was back on the golden lotus, meditating upon the holy name of the Lord.

For some reason, he was finding it difficult to concentrate and his mind kept wandering to the man who had created an entire star system to rival his own creations. He wasn't insecure, for he knew no one could attain the position of Brahma that easily, yet he couldn't help but feel a little envious of the ease with which Vishwamitra had performed the remarkable feat.

His four foreheads creased in a frown and he finally opened two of his eyes in impatience, beholding the newly formed planets that were being ruled by Satyavrat. There was no doubt that they were a work of art but his astute mind realized that their creation had also served another important purpose. Indra's inflated ego had been put in place and the Devas had been made to realize that even though they possessed god-like qualities, they were not God themselves.

He shifted his vision to glance at the latest Brahmarishi and found him meditating in the Himalayas, creating new verses and biding his time for the perfect apprentice to whom he could impart all this knowledge. Brahma knew that time was not far, for the Asurs were growing in power under their ruler

Ravan, another of his great-grandsons gone astray. With some exasperation he thought that only Narayan could know how the minds of this younger generation worked!

He himself had spent fifty years trying to balance out the Good and Evil in this world by intermittently helping one or the other side, but the contest between them never seemed to come to a final conclusion.

His gaze wandered to the other living beings on Earth and he saw tiny ant-like humans going about their usual chores, completely oblivious to the greatness one of their own had managed to achieve. Living in a world they had modified immensely for their comfort, they seldom realized what they were capable of achieving.

Unfortunately, the Devas were no better. They lived in unimaginable bliss but, ironically, this very happiness was keeping them away from Nirvana for it blinded them to the limitations of this material creation. They lived as if they had all the time in the world when the truth was that even their incredibly long lives would come to an end sooner or later.

Asurs possessed superhuman powers but were largely consumed by the insatiable desire for supremacy over the world. Most of their time was spent hoarding wealth, winning new territories and other hedonistic pursuits, putting the thought of liberation at the very end of their pleasure-seeking minds.

Both, however possessed powers that could never be matched by an ordinary human. Yet, humans were the only species that was a perfect blend of Good and Evil. They represented the exact midpoint of the evolutionary ladder and were uniquely placed to take on the traits of either side of the spectrum. Yet, they wasted their lives consumed by their unrequited desires and regrets.

He could count on one hand the number of humans who had dared to delve into the deeper recesses of their subconscious and was proud of the progress Vishwamitra had made even though he knew that, in times to come, mankind would wonder if such a man had really existed and if his stupendous achievements were actually based on fact.

He sighed deeply, realizing how terribly tiring the web of Karma was. Perhaps he hadn't been such a good Creator but then he had had no previous experiences to learn from. Who knew, maybe the next Brahma would do a better job than him.

He had another fifty years of trial and error and he hoped the second half of his life would turn out to be more positive. The twenty-fourth Mahayug of the first day of his fifty-first year was dawning and he looked forward to what lay ahead.

It was time to begin the beginning, all over again.

Acknowledgements

To every individual in this world, his own work seems quite compelling, yet the law of averages would beg to differ from our own self-assessment. You may have liked my work or hated it completely, but the story shared in this book reflects my own conviction, that mankind can do much better than the state it currently finds itself in.

The journey to this book has taken a long, winding path, beginning years ago with me as a child lapping up fantastical stories told by my kindly grandmother before she lost her voice to a stroke. I was captivated by her beautiful name, Yashoda, and imagined myself as her own personal Krishna whom she loved to pamper.

My grandfather retired as the headmaster of a high school and was already a well-known author by the time I was born, with books on history and geography to his credit. Yet, true to his name, Jugal, he never lost the sense of adventure that youth entails and encouraged all his grandchildren to define their own journeys.

Their unique combination of tradition tempered with scientific fact fostered in me a fascination for the past and set me on the path whose culmination is the book that you, my reader, currently hold in your hands.

My father was the second storyteller in our family, sharing with us bedtime tales of the sun and moon who would take the form of paternal and maternal uncles in our imagination. A renowned surgeon, devoted to his craft and his patients, he would still find time to weave a web of truth and fiction for us every night. He also made sure that we learnt about our culture and history through those fabulous comics of our childhood—the Amar Chitra Katha series that children today, unfortunately, seem completely unaware of. Every weekend my sister and I would be presented with one book each that we would greedily finish and exchange so that we could be rewarded with two more on the coming Saturday. Behind this effort was the honest desire to give the children he loved a good upbringing and in more ways than one my father has proved himself true to his name—Satish.

It was, however, my mother Kiran who, like the proverbial ray of light, showed us by personal example what complete and total dedication to family meant. Her family had been uprooted from their centuries-old home at the time of Partition, but nevertheless, or perhaps because of that, they laid more stress on the goodness of human conduct than blind following of religious diktats and personal ambition. Like many women from the previous generation, she sacrificed her own career to take care of her ailing in-laws, a never-ending stream of visitors and two troublesome children without complaint. While my father focused on studies as per the curriculum, she encouraged our artistic inclinations, inculcating in us a healthy appreciation for what were termed 'extra-curricular' activities in the school lexicon.

My school was perhaps where this journey reached its first milestone for it was within its red-brick walls that I learnt the value of creating a balance between personal and professional life. We were fortunate to learn from teachers who, instead of confining us to our textbooks, let our imaginations soar and helped us see the bigger picture. That was where I wrote my first prose.

My sister Vandana is the first person I knew of personally who could paint a picture with minimum words. She spun them into strings of such splendour that I found myself envious of her at first, and then inspired to take the pen in my own hand and attempt to create my own works of art.

Throughout college life I encountered many people who helped knowingly and otherwise by adding their own perspectives to the narrative. As I look back, I realize the influence each of the above have had on me as a storyteller and thank them for moulding me into the person I am today.

My love of science and affection for mythology ultimately found common ground in Decode Hindu Mythology, my blog. I am grateful to the electronic medium that provided me with an outlet where I could pour the swirling thoughts in my head into coherent articles that have delighted close to a million people till date. I thank everybody who has taken time out to visit and comment on my posts and encouraged my efforts.

The blog put me in touch with many like-minded people including Vaishali and Shatarupa, my editors and guides in this journey. Vaishali has been instrumental in bringing this book to fruition and has at various times cajoled, bullied, entreated and argued with me in order to get the final version ready on time and I can't thank her enough. Shatarupa has moulded my incoherent sentences into a smooth-flowing stream and her effort is visible in each page of the book.

I also thank my publisher for giving me the opportunity to present my interpretation of the events of a bygone era, for what is the value of a story if it does not reach an audience.

I am grateful to all my friends who have encouraged me throughout this endeavour—Umang, Saurin, Mihir, Jayati,

Anuj, Shoaib, Harsh, Seema, Anand, Mausam, Shagun, Vipin, Sonu, Yousaf, Avimanyu, Rajat, Anurag and Suhail. I owe you all heartfelt gratitude for making me believe I could do it.

Last but definitely the most important, I thank you, my reader, for fulfilling my journey and becoming its final destination. You can reach me through my blog—www.decodehindumythology.blogspot.com—and Facebook page—www.facebook.com/Dr.Vineet.Official—and I promise to respond to each and every thought that you may want to share.

I conclude with an invocation from the Rig Veda that sums up the philosophy of my life:

आ नो भद्राः क्रतवो यन्तु विश्वतः
Aa no bhadrah kratvo yantu vishvatah

Let noble thoughts come to us from all over the globe
Aum Shanti: Shanti: Shanti: